BOUND BY ELEMENTS

CHLOE O'CONNOR

BOUND BY ELEMENTS

The Elemental Series
Prequel

By Chloe O'Connor

To my beautiful sons, Edward & Harry.
This one is for you, my sweet boys!

Content Guidance

A note from the Author:

I do not recommend anyone under the age of eighteen to be reading this book.

Violence
Death
Sexual content
Coarse language

Please note: I will not be apologizing for writing this book.

ARCHURILLIA
AMAROK
Academy of Elements
Flamemond
FIRE COURT
EARTH COURT
Clearhill
AIR COURT
Mossmain
Ebonwater
WATER COURT
Baysummit
PHOENIX
SERPANT
OUROBOROS
REALM OF INIXIAM
GRIFFIN
N
E
S
W

Chapter One

Arthur

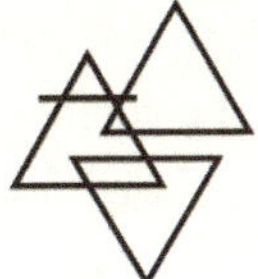

Two thousand years ago, before the great war against humans began.

"Arthur, will you come inside for dinner now?" My wife calls from the entrance of our hut. Our home.

"Coming my love," I call back. I just want to watch the sun go down, knowing exactly what tomorrow will bring. The routine of our lives, the mundane of everything, is just perfect.

I don't think I can cope with anything out of the usual routine.

Turning my back to the sunset, I walk inside the hut to find my wife and daughter sitting at the table with their plate of dinner in front of them. Taking my seat next to Mary and opposite Delilah. Reaching across the table, I clasp my hand with both of theirs, bowing my head. I speak the words, feeling the instant power flow within my entire being.

"Thank you to our Guardians for the power we are blessed with, our food that we are able to grow on these lands, and our peaceful way of living."

I let go of Mary's and Delilah's hands, bringing mine to my lips. I kiss my hands in thanks and smile toward the sky.

The warmth from my power zings; it's like the Guardians are saying thanks back.

No one has ever seen them; they are just legends from what has been written in the history books, but I know deep down they are there. Out there, somewhere. Watching us, keeping the balance between good and evil.

Doing the nightly routine after dinner, we tuck Delilah into her bed. She always has one question for me or Mary. It's how it's always been, and tonight isn't any different.

"Father, if you could pick your power, what would you choose?" What a thought-out question. I wonder what brought this question to her mind. Does she not like being a Water Fae, like her mother and me?

"What brought this question on, my daughter?" I question her. Taking a seat next to her on the bed. From the corner of my eye, I watch Mary lean against the doorframe, watching us and staying silent.

"If you didn't have waterpower, what would you like to have instead? I know I would love to control the wind!" She beams. I've never really considered another power except the one I was born with.

"Have you asked your mother the same question?"

"Of course, but she was waiting for your answer first. Are you going to answer me?" She huffs out a breath of air.

"Why aren't you curious? It's not hard to think about what it would be like to have another power."

"I don't know, maybe it's a blessing already that we can harness any power at all. There are humans out in this realm that can't harness power, and I have heard stories about them wishing to do so." She sinks deeper into the bed.

"I would hate that." Sadness takes over her expression, deep in thought.

"It's how the world works, my sweet daughter." I stand from sitting beside her bed, bending down, I give her a kiss on the head.

"Goodnight."

"Night, father."

* * *

Lying in bed several hours later, staring up at the ceiling I feel the bed shift beside me.

"Why are you up so early?" Mary places her hand on my shoulder and stares at the ceiling, with me.

"Have you slept at all?" She asks me, and I can feel the worry in her tone of voice.

"No, I couldn't get to sleep."

"That's unusual for you." I nod in agreement. It is.

"Delilah's question before threw me a little bit. I haven't really thought about what it would be like to harness another power other than my own. There shouldn't even be a thought on the matter, or at least I thought there wouldn't be... until tonight." I never really thought I wanted to control more than water, not as having two powers at once, but more like having control; of a different power other than being born with the power to control water.

To control fire would be too out of control, the Fae are hot-headed and unpredictable at best. I think that would be a nightmare power to have. Unless you were already born with it, then you really don't have a choice...

Air power would be an easy option to control, considering - air and the wind. It feels light and calming, and it is something I could consider, again, if I was given the choice.

To be an Earth Fae, it would honestly be refreshing and would suit Mary more than myself. To feel grounded within the land you stand on to feel like Mother Nature has blessed you. That would be something else.

Waterpower. That's my home, that's what I belong to.

To explain what controlling water is for me, it's the calm, the coolness within my veins. That's the reason I chose to build our hut, our home, closer to the ocean. The three of us have better strength when we are closest to the primary water source - the ocean.

"Don't let her question stir you; she is only a child and is a very curious one at that. Try and get some sleep." She pats her hand over my chest. Trying to comfort me to sleep.

I take in the fact that she lies next to me, my wife, my entire world.

My eyelids slowly begin to close.

Sleep soon takes me, and it comes with peace.

Chapter Two

Mary

Fifteen years since we built and settled into our hut. Our home.

I always saw myself with multiple children running around the field playing together. Enjoying each other's company, putting the sibling rivalry to the test, but I'm collecting herbs with my miracle child instead. Delilah.

Arthur and I had been trying for a child for many years, and I was so close to giving up, to throw in the towel, when the following week I fell pregnant. We didn't even attempt to try again after her; we knew Delilah would be an only child, and we would put every effort into her.

Seeing her, collecting herbs in our garden is therapeutic to the mind.

I have some knowledge of what each plant can be used for. Some more potent herbs can be used for healing cuts and deeper wounds. Can assist with headaches or stomach aches. Less potent herbs are good for flavouring our meals, giving it a bit more flavour to the bland food we grow on our lands.

I have taught everything I know to her and my niece Daisy.

"Mother, can I harvest the fruits today?" Delilah asks me as she proceeds to take a basket from my hands.

"Of course, but please take Daisy with you. I don't want you going on your own just yet."

"What are you worried about, mother? There is literally no one around for miles!" Her voice was loud, loud enough for the closest birds to fly away.

"Tone, young lady." I hear her groan under her breath.

"There could always be travellers, and I've heard there have been some trouble in the midlands with the villagers. I don't want to bring that kind of trouble here."

"The chance of that happening is slim, and you know I will always be careful. Run if I must." She crosses her arms over her chest, the basket dangling by her fingers close to her side.

Children, they think they know best. I wish I could go an afternoon without her attitude.

"Just do as you're told. You are only eleven years old."

"Just know, this isn't fair," She huffs, "Come on, Daisy." She takes Daisy's hand and walks away from me. Daisy is only eight and needs support. She doesn't talk much since her mother died, my sister. Guardians watch her soul. I look up to the sky and send a silent message to her. Touching the empty space in my chest where her love bloomed, it's now since empty. It's been a rough five months. I'm hoping Delilah can help Daisy come out of her shell a bit more.

"Was your mother ever this bossy?" I hear Delilah ask Daisy.

"Sometimes," Daisy replied.

There conversation grew distant the further they walked away from me.

A few minutes have passed, and the crunch of grass and twigs stops me mid-collection of some mushrooms. I look up and see Arthur approaching.

"Come on, my love, there is a storm brewing, and I need an extra hand to secure everything down."

"I've just sent the girls off to collect fruits." I knew I shouldn't have sent them away.

"The girls will be fine. Once Delilah gets bored picking fruit, and we both know she will, she'll come home." That doesn't squash my worry. Nothing will, not until I go out there to bring them both back home.

Daisy has been staying with us for the last five months. Her father hasn't been the same since my sister's death. I don't blame him, and honestly, neither have I. I can't dwell too long on my emotions because I must put on a brave face for both girls.

I know one day he will come back to collect Daisy, and I'll be waiting for that day, as I'm sure Daisy will too. It would be extremely hard for her, being without her mother is one thing, but for your father to walk out like that. No wonder she isn't speaking much right now.

Arthur takes my hand in his, and we walk hand in hand back to our home. I've been daydreaming of our forever, and this bittersweet feeling.

"How would you feel about having another baby?" Arthur stops dead in his tracks. Going completely still, he drops my hand and slowly turns to face me.

I can't read his face from that angle.

"I..." He pauses, trying to find the right words. Seeing him struggle is breaking my heart.

"Are you sure?" There is no emotion in his tone. None. Shit.

I knew I shouldn't have said anything, but seeing

Delilah with Daisy triggered something within me. I knew after having Delilah, I swore off having any more children. But what if Delilah has been yearning for a sibling? Could I live with the fact that she missed out on having someone? I know Daisy isn't a sibling, she's her cousin, but maybe it's the companionship she didn't get to have, and Daisy will eventually return to her father.

"I thought we had discussed this." We start walking again, but we aren't hand in hand. My heart hurts from the lack of contact.

"We have, but will I regret not having another? Can I be content with our daughter until my dying breath? Would I always yearn for another? These are the questions I want answered before it's too late."

He stops again, grabbing me by the waist and spinning me around to face him once more.

"My love, there is no more room for another now that Daisy is living with us. We both agreed even before that, that Delilah would be our only child. That it was too risky for you. I couldn't bear to lose you, my love for you is eternal, please know you are enough, in this lifetime and to the next." Searching my eyes, he's hoping to see that I will let this matter go. He inhales a deep breath and lets my waist go.

I put on a brave face and nod. Knowing deep down, I wish this wasn't the outcome.

"You're right, I love what I have right now, and that is enough. It should be enough." Exhaling a long, deep breath.

The instant heartache returns. I could go days without this feeling arising in my chest, but for some reason, today it's really killing me.

These thoughts about wanting another child, even though I know the costs, and risks I would have to take, is truly great, but I can't seem to shake it away. Normally, I would, and I would continue with my day without anyone realising anything was amiss with me.

"You are enough, in my eyes, my love." Arthur's sweet voice breaks through my spiral.

I mentally shake away the thoughts of another child, the thought of another sweet baby to love and to adore. To watch Delilah become a big sister. I will always mourn what could have been.

Arthur silently steps toward me, he gently wipes away a tear that has escaped my eye.

"My love, everything will be okay." He leans down and kisses my forehead.

I lean into his embrace, soaking up his warmth and love. If only he knew my true ache, deep down in my bones that I was put on this solid ground to love, and to love fully.

That is what I shall do, with Arthur, with Delilah and with Daisy until my last dying breath.

Chapter Three

Arthur

The walk back to the hut was filled with silence. I can sense the storm is just about to hit us. Mary and I hurry to tighten down the hatches, tying down loose haybales for the horses, putting netting over the veggie patches and anything that loose will blow away in the strong winds, which is fast approaching.

The girls arrived home not long after us.

"How much longer? I'm getting scared." Daisy asks me, coming to stand beside me, looking out the locked and secured window.

"In the next half an hour. I'm afraid to say but the worst is yet to come." I place my hand on her shoulder and give it a light squeeze.

"I think you and Delilah need to go and stay in your rooms." She nods in agreement.

"Arty, I haven't seen a storm this bad before." Mary comes to stand where Daisy once was.

"Neither have I, my love. We will just have to stay together, and hope it doesn't take the hut." I wrap my arm around her waist and pull her tight against my side.

She takes comfort in my arms and leans into my embrace.

"Should we try harnessing our power to have less of a chance of flooding and water damage?" I've thought about it, and I don't want to risk it. Using our powers like that could have a negative impact on the realm. I don't want to be the cause the villagers come for us.

I know some of them have a temper.

"Let's just wait and see how bad it gets before we resort to our gifts." I lead us away from the window and to the next room, where the girls are playing.

An hour in, the storm is at its peak, and I'm even convinced the roof of the hut is about to blow away. I've never seen these strong winds before.

The windows I had to board up an hour into the storm are now open and flapping like mad in the wind.

I think it's time.

I know using my power will have consequences, but I must. It's for the safety of the girls. I would risk a thousand and more storms to keep them safe.

And to hell to the villagers, if they catch wind of what's happened here, I'll gladly take the consequences.

I lean over and kiss all three girls on their foreheads.

Whatever happens, I want them to know that was the last memory they will have of me.

Turning the wooden door handle of the hut, the wooden door opens. The crunch of leaves under my feet is the only sound I hear besides the howling wind. The rain welts against my face, my hands become cold, and my clothes start to soak through.

Tilting my head to the sky, slowly closing my eyes, I

begin to feel it. I embrace the wetness of the water around me, feeling it touch my skin, and the power within my vein's buzzes to life.

This... this is what I'm meant to do. I know I'm meant for more.

To be of greatness, someone who's bound by elements. To be more than a farmer, a man who stays at home and fathers the girls.

With my eyes closed, I will the rain to ease, making it slow to tiny droplets. Drip, drip... against my face. It doesn't take long for it to reduce to nothing. I open my eyes to see that the rain has stopped, but the wind doesn't let up. Instead, it's taken another turn... for the worse.

I'm finding it harder and harder to keep my feet planted on the ground.

It doesn't take long before my clothes are dry; I have this wind to thank. My feet start to drag in the dirt; I can't keep still. It's impossible now. I can't go back inside - not like this. There isn't any way I can get the wind to stop. It's not my power; I can't control air, but if I don't go back inside, I will be lost forever...

This isn't how my story ends... I look to my left of the entrance to our hut and grab onto a piece of rope tied to the timber.

Closing my eyes like I've just done. I feel the wind on my face, the cool air sweeping over my skin, and something suddenly sparks inside me.

It's like a tornado swirling around inside, going from my head down to my toes. This feeling is different from when I harness water, this is new... this is.... something...

I picture the wind slowing down, willing it to calm and disappear.

Thinking of only calm days where the sun shines through the barely visible clouds.

I feel the wind ease, but it's still going around my entire body.

Knowing this is my last chance to get it under control. I will the wind to stop, forcing every bit of energy I feel within my body.

Finally, it obeys.

Opening my eyes, I look around my land.

Gone.

The rain, the wind, and the dark black clouds that covered the sky... gone.

What just happened?

Surely it wasn't me, but as soon as the wind resides, the power within me dies down, but I can still feel it. The brightness within me still simmers, like I can still reach out, and touch it.

What does this mean?

'Ahhh. Greatness you will be.'

A voice. I spin around where I'm standing, but there isn't anyone there. I'm completely alone. Where did it come from?

"Arty, is it safe to come out now?" I hear Mary call from inside the hut.

"Yes, my love, everything is fine now." Mary and the girls' footsteps approach closer, and I can hear the sigh of relief from my beloved wife.

"I can't believe you did it!" She beams, if only she knew to the extent of it. I will not tell her the truth that... I'm still trying to grasp myself. Did I harness air?

That has never been heard of, let alone to actually harness a second element.

'You are meant for greatness.'

It's the voice again.

"Arty?" The concern in Mary's voice brings me back down to focus on the now.

"I'm okay."

"Are you sure? You look tired." I take her hand in mine, kissing her palm and smiling.

"Perhaps I am." Leaning closer, I kiss her forehead. Maybe a lay-down is what I need. To clear my mind and body from what happened in that storm.

Chapter Four

Arthur

"Arthur! Arthur! Wake up!" Mary's voice is frantic; my entire body is shaking from Mary's hands. It pulls me out of my deep slumber.

"What... what is it, my love?" I slowly sit up in bed, groggy from the deepest sleep I've ever had, yet I don't feel rested. Looking around the room in our hut, there doesn't seem to be anything out of the ordinary.

"You have been asleep for three days!!" She sits on the end of the bed, shaken and slightly away from me. It's almost like she doesn't want to be near me.

"That can't be right. Why haven't you tried to wake me earlier?" I reach out for her, and she flinches, but only the slightest.

"I have; this is the first time you've awoken. Something isn't right here, Arthur. You haven't done this before, and it's only after you went out into that storm! How much of your power did you use?" I never told her the events that happened during that storm... and I never will.

"I used the same amount, as any other time I have used my power... You know that." She won't even look at me now.

I wish I could tell her, but will she fully understand? I wish I knew.

"Something is different, Arthur; I can feel it." She finally looks at me to emphasize her words.

"I only used the small amount of power to ease the rain..." It's not exactly a lie; I did use my power on the rain...

The smallest gust of wind whirls around us.

"Did you feel that?" Mary rushes out her words.

"No." Of course I did, but I can't let Mary know that.

"I swear I felt something, did the wind last night lift a panel off the roof? Are we getting a draft in here, somewhere?"

I look around the room and shake my head.

"Hmm, well, since you aren't unwell or dead. You can do the fruit harvest today." She stands, wiping her hands on her apron, and storms out of our room.

I've never seen Mary this mad before. I don't know what has gotten into her. Yes, I used my power; no, she doesn't know anything else that happened in that storm, and she never will. I can't wrap my mind around the fact that I slept for three days.

I hate lying to her, but I know something is wrong.

Something is seriously wrong.

'You are adjusting, give it time.'

It's that voice again, looking around the room, but I've come up empty. There isn't anyone here.

Am I going crazy?

'Crazy is for the weak, weak you are not.'

I don't waste any daylight, I get out of bed, put my boots, on and make my way to the fruit trees. Maybe if I do something so repetitive, it'll ease my mind.

I'm halfway across the fields and making sure I look

around to make sure there isn't anyone close by. I take this opportunity to try to use air power again.

Closing my eyes, I feel the connection I have to water and feel the buzz beneath my skin. I try to feel my way to a different kind of magic... the same feeling I had in the middle of the storm.

Nothing.

I don't feel anything different, besides my power connected to water. I continue my journey to the fruit trees, not wasting any more daylight.

I've got my trusty basket in hand and walk to the nearest fruit tree. Apple trees.

These ones are the green apples. They are Delilah's favourite, so I make sure I harvest plenty of them for her and for the trade market.

Stepping toward the nearest apple tree, looking up, I spot three large, round apples high up in the branches. There is no way I will be able to get them down. The girls usually climb the trees to get the really high ones. Today, I'm on my own.

What can I do to try and take these apples down? I know I tried to use air power before, but I couldn't summon it. I want to try again. This time, really dig deep and concentrate on the air around me.

Setting the basket down at my feet, I raise both of my hands and point to the branch closest to me. The one that has the most apples.

Staring at the apple, I let open the flood gates to my power and feel the zing of electricity, the hum of power within me. Two different feelings are stirring there; I can feel it now. The water is consistent, flowy, and what feels like home, and then there is the windy, wavy flow of air. I grab onto that and harness it. In my mind, I picture the air plucking the apple from the tree and gliding it down to the basket.

I smile; this seems easy enough...

Or so I thought...

The apple detached with a snap from the branch it was hanging from and fell fast, right down to the grass below.

Shit.

This is going to be harder than I thought.

I mean, at least I got it to snap off the branch.

Closing my eyes, I really try to concentrate on moving the apple through the air. I attempt it again, this time focusing more on the landing rather than pulling the apple off the branch.

The apple detaches from the tree and its floating mid-air.

I can't believe my eyes. It's truly happening!

It floats down, and hits the halfway mark, and drops again.

Shit.

At least I'm making some kind of progress.

Now, to focus more on the landing.

I spot another apple, the last one high in the tree. and closing my eyes once more, I concentrate on the web of power within my body.

My eyes shoot open when I hear the apple snap off the branch, - hovering in the air, seeing it slowly float down, just before it gets to the halfway mark. I change my thoughts; I focus more on the landing in the basket and plonk. The apple lands in the middle of the basket.

Yes!

I jump up, my feet leaving the ground, and fist the air.

I did it!

'Greatness'

The voice comments.

"If you are here, come out and say it to me..." I say into the open field, feeling stupid.

Silence.

I can never tell Mary or the girls about this. Word can't get out about this additional gift. If it did, we wouldn't be safe. The villagers would deem me a threat, and they would either try to get me to leave our home or, worse, they will try to kill me or even my family.

I couldn't risk that. That's why this is my greatest secret.

After an hour, I'm wiped. I've collected enough apples by using my power. The light in the sky is just about to run out. I know it's time to head back home. Hopefully, Mary will be pleased with my harvest and talk to me.

The sun setting and the land before me is absolutely stunning. The flowers are just about to bloom, and the little patch of Daffodils are Mary's favourite. When we married, we both promised we would forever lay to rest in this field together.

I can see my tiny hut lit up the night sky.

There's something off...

Quickly turning around from where I've walked, looking around the empty fields to see no one there. I don't know why I suddenly got this feeling of someone watching me.

Strange.

Danger.

That's the feeling I've got creeping up the back of my neck.

Chapter Five

Florin - Griffin

"Are you doing, okay?" Ameria's large frame casts a shadow over where I'm resting. Striding over, she stands directly in front of me

"No." I shift my wings, stretching them out to either side of my body.

Trying to release the tension within the muscles of my wings.

"I can sense... magic." She takes a step closer to me, making sure that she's directly in front of me.

Bowing her head, she inhales a deep breath. Huffing out a heated, thick, black smoke. I know this move; she's suspicious of something. I strain my neck to look up at her.

I have always been in awe of her, our leader. She represents strength, courage, and intelligence - The true meaning of a warrior.

"There is something there," she goes on to tell me, "I can feel the vibration coursing through my body, but I can't explain it. It's not the usual magical pull I have; this is new... like there's a connection reaching out to something... to someone..." She tilts her head, like she's getting a better look at me. Inspecting me closer, she lowers her head further down, so we are now eye to eye.

"I can see the strands of magic flowing from your body." I don't say anything with her this close.

Inspecting the strands of magic only she can see, but I know I can feel.

"Did you do something out of the ordinary?"

"No," I reply. Finally able to find my voice.

"I'll speak with the others, in the meantime... leave it be. Don't go and provoke it..." She stands back, her enormous black wings spread wide, and without a second thought, she takes flight.

I know I should listen to her, but I am a curious being...

Closing my eyes, I start to feel the magic strands within my core, and I begin to follow the path...

The connection is extremely far away. I follow it across the oceans, and when I've reached land, it takes me to a small village by the water's edge. I follow this magical thread all the while staying grounded, staying where I'm supposed to.

My mind draws closer and closer to the threads end, and there!

I can just make it out...

A human!

That can't be, humans don't and can't possess magic. There must be a mistake. There must be some kind of mistake. The balance as we know it will be forever changed.

I need to tell Ameria before she talks to the others...

She must know before they do; she must think of a plan before alerting the others.

Quickly opening my eyes, I open my mind to our connection, the magic line we all share. The only way we can communicate from a distance. Mind links. A bond.

'Ameria.' I call out her name.

"What is it Flyran?" Ameria hisses down the bond.

"I think it's a human…" The quick inhale of her breath isn't mistaken.

"What have you done!" The rage shoots down the magical bond.

Well, shit, she's pissed.

I'm glad no one else can tap into our bond and hear this heated conversation. I think everyone else would be pissed, too. At me.

"I haven't done anything!! I stayed put like you ordered me to, I just followed the link telepathically. The magic seems to be tied to this being…" I don't want to fly to her; that would show my weakness. I have not done anything wrong; I will not yield.

"Stay where you are, and for the love of the Guardians, don't do it again. I'm coming back to you." Ameria breaks the bond with a snap, so I can't reach out to her anymore.

Great.

It's not long before Ameria reappears in front of me, she huffs hot steam from her nose straight into my face. She's pissed.

So, pissed.

"Flyran, tell me what you did to discover this magic link?" I know deep down it's a bond forged, but I won't tell her that… not yet anyway.

"I just followed it like I would with you or the others. The same way we communicate, our link to one another." She tilts her head, studying what I've just told her.

"If that is true, then we can bond with the humans… the Fae."

"Fae?"

"Yes, you idiot, the Fae are beings who can harness

power, the elements... the humans are just that. Non-magical beings, did you bond with a human or a Fae?" She hasn't exactly pieced it together yet, but I'm sure she will get there.

It is no wonder the human felt different; this being vibrated with magic - something I've never experienced before.

"So, I've been linked to a Fae?"

"Yes. Flyran, don't be so naive. You aren't just linked to this Fae being. You are bonded. Just like you and I are." She's lost in thought for a second. "I always thought this was possible, to be bonded with the Fae, but to see it proven, well, it's a miracle."

"When do I get to meet this, Fae?" I didn't get a closer look at this Fae being. I didn't want to go over the edge and have Ameria's wrath directed at me... I do wonder what they are like. How they live, what other type of magic they can harness, and most importantly... what they look like.

"Soon enough. You need to learn patience now, Flyran. The first task for you now is to learn how to cut off half of your magic. Dim the flow to a low dosage, connecting to the Fae. Otherwise, if they harness too much power from you, you could burn out and die."

"I didn't think it was possible for us to die..." We are the pure essence of the power source in Inixiam.

"Anything has a means to die, Flyran... even us." Well, that's a bit morbid.

"Life, Flyran. Such is life." She turns away from me.

Spreading her enormous black wings, her dagger tail swishing in the air, turning to me, she says, "Not a word to the others. Let me tell them first. This kind of news needs to come from me. I know how to calm each of them. We do not want a riot on our hands, at least not right now." She takes a step away from me and stops in her tracks, turning back to me.

"Go to this connection, observe them. Do not interact with this being. I want a full report."

Nodding my head in agreement, she flaps her wings and takes off into the night sky.

How in the world can I obey her? Knowing everything I do right now I am anticipating meeting this Fae I am not bonded to. I am surprised she took that well... unless it was all an act, and I'm now waiting for the other scale to drop...

Chapter Six

Arthur

Mary's punishment for harvesting fruit would usually be just that... punishment. Harvesting fruit is more of a chore some days, but other days, it can be good.

With my newfound power, I've been enjoying it more and more...

I'll never tell Mary that.

Most days, while harvesting the fruits, I'll use my air power, and when the day is nearing its end, I am beyond boned tired. My wife thinks it's due to working long hours in the fields. If only she knew...

'You've gotten good with your new power.'

It's that voice again.

Turning around in the field, there isn't anyone in sight.

No one. Just pure silence.

Crack.

Turning quickly around on the spot, I notice the large, dark shadow beside one of the tallest apple trees. Hiding from eyesight, I'm hesitant to move, to inspect the shadow closer.

"Come out, whoever you are!" I yell, gaining the courage to speak.

'Not yet.'

The voice chuckles. I can't figure out if this person is saying the words out loud or if this creature is somehow communicating in my mind.

Crack.

Hearing that sound again, I can only assume another branch snaps from a nearby tree. I take a step backward; the threat sounds huge. Not liking the closeness of the sound of that last tree branch breaking, or how loud it was. Sounding like *something* heavy broke it, not some mere villager.

'Are you scared yet?'

The voice asks me. It's toying with me, beckons me to answer.

Great.

"No!" I lie.

'Silly Fae. You shouldn't lie to me, Great One. I can hear your thoughts and feel your intentions.'

Fuck.

I don't swear often and don't use that word lightly, but in this moment, I am scared shitless.

"Please don't hurt me." My voice, shaky from fear.

'I could never, even if I wanted to.'

Another crack.

It's getting closer and closer, still within the shadows of the trees.

"What are you doing here then? Why do you keep communicating with me?" I shout to wherever they are.

'Because I am bonded to you.'

"Bonded?" I ask.

'Yes.'

The voice is always so close; it must be within my thoughts.

Crack.

I quickly spin around at the last tree branch snapping. It came from behind me. Taking in the sight before me, I lost any breath I had inhaled seconds ago. Before me is standing this enormous creature.

'Hasn't anyone ever told you what we are? Us creatures are the power you harness?'

The creature stands taller, like it's showing itself off to me.

"I've heard rumours of mythical creatures, six in total, who power our realm, but they are just that... rumours."

'Do I look like a rumour?' Cocking its head to the side.

"No..." My legs are becoming shaky, and my inner fight or flight mode is in overdrive. It won't make up its mind on what it wants to do.

'Don't be scared of me, we are bonded for life.'

"That doesn't reassure me, not one bit."

'I see.'

"What are you?" I ask the creature. Do I really want to know the answer to that?

'Where are my manners? I always get told off by the others. They always say the same thing to me, where have my manners disappeared to? Did they get lost when I was created?

I'm Flyran, I am a Griffin. I've been created as half an eagle and half a lion. You see, I am one of six magical creatures, but you'll know us as mythical creatures. I am the one who over- sees Air Element with my magic linked to the

sky. We also take guard over the realm, not just this land... Archurillia.'

I ponder on his words for a hot minute.

A griffin.

The details of what I've been told from passing generations of what a griffin looks like aren't wrong. Flyran is as tall as the treetops. He has the body, the tail, and back legs of a lion and the head, wings, and front legs of a bird, the eagle. He looks magnificent.

His fur and feathers are golden brown, his claws and beak are a midnight black, and his eyes are a striking blue. Blue like the sky on a cloudless day.

"I am a water wielder. Why am I bonded to an air guardian?"

'That I'm unsure of. You'll have to speak to our leader, Ameria. She is all-knowing, most of the time,' he laughs.

"What is Ameria?"

'She is a dragon. There is also Samundra; she's a Sea Serpent, Helia; she's the one and only Phoenix, Rymaro; he's the Amarok, and Otto, who's the Ouroboros.'

"Wow." I don't have the words, even if I tried to come up with any, I just draw a blank.

"Do I get to meet them?"

'No.'

"Why not?" I would love to be the first person in history to meet all six mythical creatures.

'Stop calling us mythical, I'm standing right here in front of you.' he has a point.

He stands up straighter if that were possible.

"What's wrong?" I ask, looking left and right, but I don't see anyone here with us.

'Ameria, she's calling for me. If she found out I came to meet you without her, she is going to be extremely pissed.' he untucks his wings, gives them a flap once, twice.

'Don't do anything stupid, don't get yourself killed. I'll be seeing you again, Great one,' and he takes off for the sky.

"Arthur!" Mary's voice is in the distance.

Shit.

How long have I been here?

I look down at the disregarded fruit basket, and it's empty.

Double shit.

Looking at the apple trees again, I notice a possible ten. I must try to use my power to gather all of them at once. Can I do it? There is really only one way to find out.

Closing my eyes, steadying my heartbeat. I imagine tiny silver strands from myself reaching out to all ten apples.

Once they've connected, I get the strands to unpluck the fruit and slowly lower them to the basket. Upon opening my eyes, I observe ten apples floating in the air.

I can't believe it.

I'm actually doing it!

'Great one.' Flyran's voice filters through my mind.

Chapter Seven

Arthur

Today is the long-awaited trade day in the village. This is where all the harvested fruits I've done was in preparation for today.

Our family would trade in our fruits for meat, fish, sheep wool, and anything else sold at the markets. We have the best fruit in the land, and we sometimes even have lines of customers waiting to trade or buy our fruit.

"Are you sure I can't come?" Delilah grabs one full basket of apples to help me load up the horse and cart.

"No, I must go alone. I don't know what the energy is like from the other villagers, especially from the storm. Many of them could have lost their homes, their loved ones, or even worse... their lives." I pause to look at my daughter; she is still so young and little. I don't know what I would have done if I had lost her.

"Maybe next time you can come with me." I take the basket from her hands and lift it over the side of the cart. Adding it to the fruit and vegetable baskets resting inside.

"That is not fair!" She stomps her foot on the ground.

"It doesn't need to be fair, Delilah. I've made up my

mind, stay here with your mother and Daisy." Securing the rope around the baskets, draping a sheet over the fruit, and making sure I secure that to the cart.

Pulling tightly, I make a triple check that nothing will blow away.

"Fine." She turns away from me and walks toward the entrance to the hut. The decision was easy to make. I don't know what lies ahead for me from the other villagers. I've heard talk from passing neighbours that my property was the only one left unscathed from the storm. The villagers aren't happy. They don't understand why...

I still stand by my decision in using my powers. I don't regret it. I saved my family and our home.

"Please be safe and come home." Mary's honey-like voice pulls me from my thoughts. She steps closer and tugs on my shirt. She pulls me closer to her. I wrap my arms around her tiny frame and lower my head to hers.

"I will, my love." Leaning down, I press my lips to hers. Soft to the touch and a sweet peach flavour coating her lips.

Regretfully pulling away from her, I walk to the horse and cart to start my journey ahead. I hate this part, leaving wife, daughter, and niece. I know I'm about to meet my fate, and I'm okay with that.

Taking the horse's reins, I climb on top of the cart.

"Ya." Flapping the reins, the horse starts walking north. We are headed straight toward the villagers' trade day.

* * *

Archurillia is a peaceful land, with no war, no one trying to claim power, and no civil fighting amongst us. It was calm, a place where we could find love, grow a family, and eventually die, returning to the land. It was home.

There are different villagers spread out amongst the land. The Fae remaining in their own elemental groups. The Fire Fae remaining in the north, the top end of the land, where they can draw power from the volcano. They can be hot-headed, given the name fire, but you rarely see any of them travel outside their walls.

The Earth Fae, remaining just south of them, form a barrier between the air and fire villagers. Air Fae and Fire Fae can mix, but it wouldn't be a good outcome. Still going south, Air villagers are where most mountains remain, and south of them are Water Fae's. Me. Living closest to the water's edge is calming, peaceful, and somewhat magical.

We sometimes get travellers passing through our land to the docks, wanting to travel on ships to try and find others from different lands, but those who leave the land, most never return. The waters are dangerous, terrifying to those who aren't Water Fae. Those who can't use their power to manipulate the waves, the current, or bargain with creatures below the surface. They've tried to bribe Water Fae to join their travels, but mostly all refuse to go. They know the risks, and it's just not worth it. Those who don't return either have found a new home, somewhere out in the beyond, or they get lost at sea. The lucky ones who have returned get to tell many tales of their journey.

You can feel the magic radiating through the ground when you walk, feel it swirling through the air with the wind, and it makes my soul come alive. I love living on this island. However, I wouldn't have any knowledge of the other islands other than what the other villages have said when they have done several voyages.

I have always wanted to travel, to go out into the sea and have the saltwater splash over my face, have the salty wind blowing through my hair, and the full power of water with me.

Instead, I decided to stay home and help raise our only daughter. Delilah.

Mary and I had chosen to do this together. Raise our Water Fae born to be the best version of herself instead of leaving that responsibility to my wife.

I couldn't do it. I couldn't miss out on the major milestones of her life, miss out on her first steps, watch her harness her power for the first time, and grow into the young, beautiful woman she would become, and eventually fall in love. No, thank you. I want to be the best father I can be for her.

She is my light. My entire world.

I made it on good time, three hours to reach the grand village.

I stopped the horse just as I see an old friend who's stopped in the middle of the road.

"It's good to see you again, Arthur." He calls out, waving his arms in the air. I didn't think I would see him here. He usually has nothing to trade; he just likes to shop.

"Goldy, pleasure is mine." Leaping down from the cart, my legs and ass hurt from sitting down for three hours straight.

"What goods have you brought?" He meets me at the side of the cart; I stretch my arms above my head and twist my hips from left to right.

"The usual, fruit, and some vegetables. It's been a good year." He asks me while clasping our forearms together. We must bring ten baskets full for the trade day. It hasn't been this good in years. We would have lost so much from the storm... but we know how that turned out.

"I'm glad to hear it, Arthur..." He takes a step closer to me, still holding of my forearm. He pulls me in close.

Within hearing distance, he says, "There have been some rumours about you..."

I slightly pull away and lift a brow. "Really?"

"Yeah, man, they have been saying you've controlled the storm to save your harvest. They've been saying you actually turned into the storm to get it to move along, and this one, yet I think is hilarious... you've turned into a mythical yourself! Can you believe these?" He laughs, a full belly laugh.

"Wow. Those are some crazy rumours. Luckily, they aren't true." I slap him on the shoulder in response.

Shit. This could turn into a manhunt. What am I going to do? Will they ever stop until they're going to prove that these rumours are true?

"I'm glad to hear it, Arthur. Please take care of yourself, you know what these villagers can do once they have a committee meeting and have an agreed outcome. I hated to see Roland and his family leave on a false accusation."

"I know, I'll be careful as you, my old friend."

"See you around." Goldy holds out his hand, I clasp his forearm, and we shake, hard. As Goldy walks away, I see a woman walking towards the cart.

"How are you, ma'am?" I ask one of the villagers' wives.

"I'm doing just fine, thank you." She has a woollen sack with her, ready to collect some fruit.

"What are you after today?" I ask her.

"Can I have a dozen apples, please?" She hands me the sack, and I pick the nicest-looking apples to go inside.

"Have you been here long?"

"No, we just got here. You are always our first stop, Arthur."

"Here you go." Smiling, I hand the sack back to her, full this time.

"Anything for your husband from the cart?" Betty and her husband grow grapes. They've experimented with the grapes and somehow turned them into a potent liquid. They've called it... wine.

It's genius.

"Anything for you?" She asks me.

"Two flasks of wine?" I reply.

"I'll go fetch it now." She walks away and leaves me standing here.

"How dare you show your face here!" Bernard stalks up to me and spits on the ground, directly at my feet.

The man is dressed in finer clothes than I am. He is wearing a black tunic with dark olive pants. His hair is brights blond and the color of the sun "What are you talking about?" This is what I feared. I didn't think Bernard would be the first to say something.

"You know damn well what I'm talking about." He takes a step closer, closing the distance between us.

"No, I've come to trade my fruit... just like you." Crossing my arms over my chest. I'm not taking anyone's shit today.

I've traded enough fruit to live off until the next trade.

I have sheep wool to make blankets for the winter, herbs for Mary to cook, and plenty of meat and fish for a while.

"Drop the act, Arthur. You are a disgrace; an abomination, and you are going to pay for what you did."

'Don't listen to that fool, you are Greatness.' Flyran's voice filters through my thoughts. I'm glad I have his confidence to rely on.

"Let me just get the two flasks of wine, and I'll leave."

"Fine. But don't dare show your face again, get your wife and that daughter of yours... what is her name?" He asks me.

"Delilah." Regret surges through the second the name slips from my lips.

Shit.

"Ah yes, Delilah..." He turns to leave, but he waits as his wife returns with the flasks.

"Here." She tosses them to me and leaves with her husband.

I can admit. It could have gone worse, but I'm glad there was no stone throwing or pitchforks at the ready. It was calmer, but there were still threats.

I pack the cart up and gather the horse's reins.

That is enough for today. I don't want to push my luck.

It's going to be another three hours until I'm back home.

I can make it. I know I can.

'Don't hesitate to defend yourself, you are Greatness.' Flyran's voice filters through again.

"Glad you have confidence in me," I murmur quietly.

'Always.'

Why is - the journey back home always quicker than when trying to go somewhere?

It did not feel like a three-hour journey.

"Father! Mother, father has returned!" Delilah greets me just before I reach the hut.

"Oh, my Arty, I'm glad you're home safe." She meets me halfway, and I wrap her tightly in my arms, soaking up her warmth and love.

"I am, my love."

Chapter Eight

Mary

"Oh, Arty, these are wonderful!" My eyes wander over all the items on the table, which are full of traded items Arthur brought back.

"You really outdid yourself this year, so far." I pick up the closest cheese to me and inhale the scent.

I sigh. It's been a long time since I have smelt, let alone tasted cheese. We usually only get back the essentials. Meat, fish, and wool. It's only if we have a really good fruit harvest that we can get other items brought back. Like cheese, herbs that I don't or can't grow, and even on the best harvest, I get a piece of jewellery.

"Anything for you, my love," Arthur whispers in my ear. The loving gesture means everything to me.

"What will you use this wool for?" Daisy dances to the kitchen table and eyes the sheep wool.

"Well, I was thinking of making some blankets for the coming winter, and possibly a blanket for the horse for those cold nights." Our old blankets have seen better days, and since Arthur just got new wool, I think it's time to upgrade them.

"That is such a good idea! Momma used to make coats for us, but it's been a long time since I've got a coat." Daisy looks sad. It's rare when she speaks of her mother, my sister. It's been too many years since I saw her.

We didn't leave things on the best of terms. In fact, if I'm being completely honest, we hated each other, and there really wasn't a reason for it. We just didn't see eye to eye, we never got along, and it only grew harder to change that when we started our own families.

"If I have enough left over, I will make sure that I make a coat especially for you." Daisy smiles so brightly; it breaks my heart in two. I'm glad that I can make this simple thing for her, but my heart hurts knowing her mother isn't here to do it herself.

"Thanks, Aunt Mary." She races up, throws her arms around my waist, and squeezes hard.

"You're most welcome, darling." I smile down at her while rubbing her back.

"Can I go meet one of my friends?" Delilah asks me.

"Arty?" I turn to my husband, watching him, as he puts all his traded items away.

"Which friend is that?" He asks her.

"Willow, you've met her before." She locks her fingers together. Something seems off about her, but I can't put my finger on it.

"Nice girl, sure, don't be home late." He doesn't look up from what he's doing.

"Thanks, Father." Delilah walks over, leans on her tippy toes, and kisses Arty's cheek.

"Wait a minute," I tell her, and she pauses.

"You can take Daisy."

"No! Mum." She stamps her foot on the ground.

"You will, end of discussion." She takes one look at Daisy and grabs her by the arm.

"You will not say anything, okay?"

"Yes. Not a word." Daisy replies.

Watching the two girls leave the hut, I take in Delilah and how she is the spitting image of her father. Sharing the same dark brown hair, blue eyes that shine bright in the sunlight, and the same chin dimple on the left side.

"Did you have to send Daisy away, too?" Arty asks me, coming up to stand behind me.

"It'll be good for Delilah to take her."

"I suppose I should thank you." He wraps one arm around my waist, and with the other hand, he displays it in front of my face.

He opens his fingers, and sitting there in his palm is a tiny brooch.

It's a hummingbird.

"Arty, it's beautiful." Taking the brooch from his hand and looking it over, side to side, inspecting how the light shines off it. "I knew you'd like it, my love." He closes his hand over mine, encasing the brooch in my palm. He turns me around and kisses me.

The type of kiss that still warms my cheeks and makes my heart flutter.

Arty breaks the kiss, only long enough to catch our breath and for him to suddenly lift me by the waist.

The sound of shock leaves my lips as he carries me to our bedroom.

The few steps it takes to get to our bedroom aren't long; he gently lowers me down onto the bed.

"By the Guardians, you are beautiful." He whispers into the air.

Standing over me, he doesn't take long before his tunic,

pants, and boots are off. Arty is now completely naked in front of me.

"Your turn." He smiles down at me.

I shift to the edge of the bed, slowly stand before him, and my eyes never leave his.

"Turn around." He leans forward and whispers the words in my ear. His lips lightly touching my skin on my neck.

I obey him, and he starts to loosen my corset laces.

The dress slowly slides off my shoulders, and I'm standing there, completely naked.

"My love, you simply take my breath away." His lips are soft against my bare shoulder.

Please let me take my time with you." He spins me around gently, guiding me back to the bed. I lay down, the soft blankets touching my heated skin, and I watch as Arthur climbs up the bed and rests over the top of me, ensuring he's keeping the weight off me.

I know this type of love can only exist in one lifetime and I am so grateful I found it in this one.

I smile up at him and count my lucky stars.

He leans down and kisses me again; this time, it's with more - urgency. It's like he needs to take his next breath, and I'm his air.

"My wife." I feel his hands travel down my sensitive skin to my breasts, going over the curves at my hips, and they stop just above my belly button.

"I could die right now and still be called the luckiest man alive." He kisses my neck right at the soft spot under my ear, and collarbone, and his lips find mine again.

My mind goes blank, and I can't form any words right now. Nothing that will be impactful in this moment.

Nothing.

Just silence.

Arthur slowly moves his hand down toward my entrance. He knows what I like, what my body craves, and he doesn't stop.

"I will never stop loving you... never."

He slowly glides one finger into my pussy and slowly strokes in and out, making sure I'm ready for him.

I match his rhythm and meet him halfway, greedy with the friction I so desperately need.

He knows me too well, and he suddenly stops right before I'm about to burst with endorphins.

Instead, he shifts higher and readies his cock at my entrance. Before I can say anything more, he pushes into me.

That instant pleasure is nothing I can ever explain. There are no words to describe that feeling. It feels like I'm floating on a cloud, but my whole body is alive and radiating with electricity.

"Arthur!" I say his name loud, fisting my hands in the blankets around us.

"I'll get you there, my love. I always do." Arthur kisses my lips softly, and he picks up his speed. The rhythm is just how I like it, not too fast and not too slow. Just right, he begins to really stroke me with his cock... in and out until we are both close to the finish line.

It hits.

And I'm in pure bliss.

The sun is setting, and I've noticed that neither of the girls are back yet.

It's been five hours since they left home to meet Delilah's friend. Yes, we said they could go, but it's getting to dinner time, and they always come home before that to help wash up.

"Arty?" I call out my husband's name; he should be outside putting the horse to bed.

"Yes, Mary?" I hear him call. Hearing footsteps getting closer to the front door.

"Have you seen the girls?" I ask him. He's been outside for an hour or so, and maybe he has seen them in the distance.

"No..." He looks toward the sky and sees the sun going down. Scratching his head, unsure of himself, he turns to me. Now I can see concern etched on his face.

"They aren't back yet." He says more to himself.

"No... I am really worried now."

"Okay. I am going to go out and look for them." He walks straight up to me and gives me a kiss on the cheek.

"I'll be back soon with the girls." He gives me another quick kiss, but on the lips this time.

"Please be safe and bring them back quickly. I don't want you out there in the dark for too long," I say, worry etched on my face and filtered through my voice.

Chapter Nine

Bernard

I knew something was wrong when I saw Arthur talking to my wife. His aurora has slightly changed around him. I have this gift alongside my earth power where I can see everyone's aurora. It mainly depends on which part of Archurillia you are from. My wife, being an earth fae she radiates green. The last time I saw Arthur, he radiated blue being a water fae but today when I saw him. He radiated a touch a grey.

That's when I knew something was wrong.

Every time I have seen Arthur, his aurora has never changed. Grey is the color of air element. That was my first clue something has happened and then the chatter I overheard just twenty minutes ago that his hut hasn't been touched by the storm, but his neighbour's had roofs missing of their barns. He manipulated air somehow and that's what I can see today.

He needs to be stopped before something bad happens to our lands.

"What's the matter dear?" My wife touches my arm

when we enter our home. The little hut along the tree line, surrounded by wildflowers and native animals.

We weren't lucky enough to have children, but my wife enjoys the native animals' company instead. I think she would prefer their company over mine sometimes... I don't blame her.

"Nothing." I smile down at her. Trying my best to convince her that there isn't, in fact anything wrong.

"Busy day trading." I reassure her, widening my smile.

"Okay, I'll make us some tea." She walks away from me at the entrance of our hut.

I need an action plan, I wonder if the other villagers noticed Arthur's presence. I know I'm the only one with this slightly other gift.

"Mary, I'm going to Gregory's hut." He is only a mile away.

"But Bernard..." She trails off when I'm already heading toward the door and out into the fresh night air.

The leaves crunch under my feet, the croaks of frogs and the flutter of birds heading to their nests for the night.

My mind is racing with anticipation and the need to do something about it. A few of the villagers have come together over the years to make a council. This council's only purpose is to protect and serve the community. In this instance, we need to act against Arthur.

I didn't waste any time getting to Gregory's hut.

"Greg!" I shouted from outside his home.

"What is the urgency Berny?" Greg opens his door and takes the step toward me, closing the distance.

"I need to rally the others, we need to have a meeting," I turn to leave but Greg takes hold of my arm, halting me in my tracks.

"What is going on?"

"There is no time to explain, we need to rally the councilmen."

"Fine." He drops my arm, and I walk to the nearby hut.

It's been an hour and there are six men standing in front of me, wondering why we are here. Concern spread across each man's face.

"What are we doing here? It's nearly the middle of the night!" Jerry calls from my right.

Taking a step forward, "I've gathered the council tonight because there is an urgent matter to our community and to our land! It is our duty as men to care for the women and children!" The crowed ushered their agreements.

"Arthur is an abomination." Throwing my hands in the air.

The room falls silent.

"That's quite an accusation Bernard." Jerry comments, not moving from his position.

"We all heard the chatter about him today, but surely it's just talk." One of the men to my right comments.

"Of course you have, we all have but I just know he isn't the Arthur we all know and care about."

"You need more evidence than that Berny." Greg says cautiously.

"I think in this instance, you all need to trust me on this. I can't prove that something has happened to Arthur, but I know by instinct."

There are low murmurs going around the room, and not one man looks at me.

Do they think I have turned mad?

I don't know how I can prove to them the knowledge I hold on Arthur. I wish I could tell them the truth about me but even then, they might think I'm the abomination too. Fuck.

"Should one of us visit him at his home? Maybe try to talk to him and see if he'll come clean about whatever this is..." Another comments.

"No! Something needs to be done now, something to show everyone who he truly is and I have just the plan..."

Chapter Ten

Arthur

I don't bother taking any supplies with me; there is no time. It's been too long since they left. This behaviour isn't like Delilah. I know she wouldn't let us worry about her and Daisy. She really does take on the older sister role very seriously.

I need to make sure they are both okay.

If only I had asked more questions about who this friend was and where they lived. I would have offered to walk them back home, kicking myself for only worrying about having some alone time with Mary.

Walking in the lands away from our hut, I'm walking directly to the fields of fruit trees. My gut is telling me that something is wrong. Coming up to the tree line, my pace starts to quicken. I round the bend leading to the first row of fruit trees and come up empty.

There is no sight of them.

Silence.

There are a few spots I can check that I know they both like to hide.

Two hours have passed and its well past sunset.

There still isn't any sign of them.

Fuck.

I can't go back home empty handed; it will destroy Mary.

Fuck.

'You are greatness.' Flyrans' voice filters through my thoughts.

"I just wish I could use my power to try and track them." I tell him, into the emptiness around me.

'You are air and water, Arthur,' he replies.

Shit. You are right...

I wonder if the power of air will allow me to track them, somehow, either guide me to where they were last or even try to find them exactly.

I have never heard of another air wielder to manifest this level of power before.

'You can do it.' Flyran's encouragement goes a long way.

Closing my eyes, I inhale a deep breath to calm my nerves and racing heart. I try to imagine the connections to both of my powers.

Water and air.

They are both tied to me. I follow the silver thread of magic and pull on it.

My entire body vibrates with power, with such certainty that it's exhilarating.

I open my eyes and feel the pull of the magic within. It's pulling me to the right of the trees, and I follow it without hesitation. Walking steadily on the grass, keeping my breathing steady.

My power starts to dim, and I notice we have reached the spot where the girls were last. Kneeling to the ground at the base of a tree, I notice scratch marks, and... there's blood.

Fuck.

There must have been a struggle.

I smooth my fingers over the droplets, they're still wet. It hasn't been long since it happened here.

Where are my girls!

I open my power back up, this time opening the flood-gates to the entire power source. I stand with rage. Somehow, I filter out my air power, and only water surges forward. It's the feeling of finally coming home - the comfort of it. Suddenly it starts to rain, and my breathing is now heavier.

'Stop the rain! Stop it now!' Flyrans' voice cancels out everything.

The full force of his power isn't mistaken. It's truly there.

The rain stops.

Shit.

I could have lost everything.

"Sorry," I mutter more to myself.

Closing off my waterpower and concentrating on air again and seeing the blood droplets have only smudged a little from the rain. I know it could have been worse if Flyran didn't help calm me down. I look down and see a little pink ribbon floating through the air. That's Delilah's. She was wearing that this morning.

I pick it out of the thin air and grasp it tightly. I can't lose her.

Not like this.

"Arthur!" A little voice comes from the corner of the tree line.

"I'm scared." The voice is so small, I can barely hear it.

Daisy!

"Daisy, is that you?" I call out into the cold night air.

"Yes." I take off, sprinting through the darkness, just mere inches from running into the fruit trees.

There, I see a small figure curled into a little ball, hiding under tiny shrubs next to an apple tree.

Crouching down, "Daisy?" I whisper into the air between us.

"Yes," barely a whisper.

I don't hesitate. She's in my arms in seconds.

"Oh, my sweet girl. What happened?" I ask her once she is safely in my arms.

"They took Delilah. She tried to fight them off, but they were too strong and there were just too many of them." Daisy shivers.

Inhaling another deep breath, I open the air's flood gates to the magic threads waiting there and let it direct me again. This time, I turn to the left and walk closer to the gravel road that connects all the properties together. The road that takes us to the main village.

I'm having this internal battle about whether to take Daisy home or go out to find Delilah. I turn around and kneel to Daisy's height.

"Do you know your way home from here?" I ask Daisy.

She nods. Still processing everything that's just happened.

"Good. I want you to run home, as fast as you can, and I don't want you stopping for anyone or anything. You got that?"

She nods again.

Kissing her on the forehead, I draw her in close.

"Now go." I give her a light nudge towards the direction of our hut and Mary.

I can't worry about Daisy right now; I have to believe she will make it back to the hut in time.

My pace picks up, my mind racing with all the thoughts that start to swirl around.

Has someone done this to my baby girl?

Has someone hurt my baby, Delilah?

My rage has returned, but I must remember to keep it in check. I can't let myself lose control like I did before. It won't benefit anyone here, especially not me.

It doesn't take me long before I reach the nearest small village. This isn't the same village that I do trading in. This is our main town, if you would call it that.

The main shops are closed and only a few drunken men wonder around. I wouldn't know the first place to look. Where is she?

The wind picks up and my clothes flap to the left, giving me a sign of where she could be. I take it as a sign, air knowing exactly who I'm looking for.

Steading my footsteps, I slowly prowl toward the hut. It's the only building with several rooms lit with a fire, and I can faintly hear, maybe four men laughing loudly.

"Can you imagine if this freak finds out we have taken his daughter?" One male comments.

"Ha, yeah. I wonder what his reaction would be. Do you think she is innocent? I would love a taste." Another voice I don't recognise.

That is my daughter! I must simmer this rage before it's too late. I must save my daughter first before letting this rage out.

"Should we go, see?" The male from before asks.

"Yes." I follow their voices to the side of the hut, and its dark inside. There is a window exposing them. I creep closer, hunching down so they don't spot me. I take a tiny look and see they have their backs to me. There, sitting on the cold floor, her hands bound, and rags shoved into her mouth. My daughter sits, scared. Her face wet from tears, and a cut just above her eyebrow.

Rage, it's simmering, and it's still not the time.

I scan the ground and find a decent-sized rock. I pick it up and throw it toward the front of the hut. Hoping the distraction will cause the men to leave the hut and give me enough time to get Delilah out of there.

The rock lands with a crack against the hut. The two men in the room with my daughter rush out of there and toward the front.

This is it.

I stand, jump in the window, and race toward my daughter.

"Shhh," I whisper in her ear. I can't let her make a sound. I can't risk them coming back inside and seeing us.

Fresh tears race down her cheeks.

"Oh, baby, I'm here." I kiss her forehead. Picking her up, she wraps her arms around my neck.

Walking quickly to the window again, I lift her out and she lands on her feet with a loud thud.

Shit.

"What was that?" One of the men rushes into the room and sees me standing by the window.

"Run!" I call out to Delilah; she freezes for a second before she takes off toward our home.

That's my girl.

"Hi." I smile a twisted, hateful smile at him.

"Arthur. Glad you could join us." The other man walks in, and it's Bernard. I can't fucking believe it.

"You took my daughter, what did you think would happen?" I shrug.

"I took you for a coward. I am never usually wrong..." He smiles at me.

"Oh, that is one thing I am not. I never let anything happen to my family - not you, not anyone. You took my daughter. Let that sink in." I take a step toward them, and they hesitate.

"I did, and you should have seen her face when I stood over her. The sheer terror on her face, it was bittersweet." I acted without thinking.

My right fist landed straight into his eye socket.

I don't feel pain.

I feel rage.

Fire.

It's burning within me.

"You shouldn't have done that!" The other guy races toward me and I just act. There was no time to think. It was all about acting in the moment.

"Oh yeah? What are you going to do about it?" I side-step their attack. He did not like that, not one bit.

This burning deep inside me is getting extremely hot... but I don't feel like I'm burning from the inside. It feels like a new power source, a new thread forming. It's something I can't explain, but it's similar to how air invaded my entire being.

Fire.

'You are Greatness' Flyrans' voice is there but faint.

Fire.

Chapter Eleven

Arthur

It happened so fast. Fire came out of nowhere. There was no way of trying to stop it. The blaze was supposed to be searing... but it wasn't burning me. The smoke- it's black and thick, and it's starting to block my view. I need to act fast; otherwise, I will be lost in here forever, and I can't leave my girls, or Mary.

I must act now.

The screams start, loud and screechy, and the shouting is coming from the men. The same men who kidnapped my daughter. It all happened so fast, the men come running into the same room I'm standing in, they start yelling... screaming... stumbling around and knocking things over. They are panicking, trying to escape.

I'm paralysed.

I can't move.

This could be my undoing.

'You need to get out of there!' Flyrans' voice demands, it shakes me out of my trance. I look around the hazy room again and see the flames wrap around the room, licking around the walls, and the ceiling. It won't take much before this entire hut will burn down. Somehow the heat of the flames isn't affecting me, it's almost like I'm a part of it, like I own the flame...

Turning around, I try to feel for the window I just came from.

There! It's three steps away from where I had just been. I lift my leg to start climbing out of it.

Fuck!

Something has a hold of my elbow.

Fuck!

"You're not getting away with this!" The gurgled screech comes from a man whose hand has a hold of my right elbow. He squeezes tightly, trying very hard not to let go of me.

He turns his body more towards me, and I see a flash of metal in front of my eyes, and then the searing pain in my left cheek endures.

Fuck!

I see a knife as the man pulls his arm back, and he's about to slice me again. I must think quick, I yank my arm out of his hold, and I push him away... hard.

He stumbles for a split second, but he regains his balance.

"I'm going to kill you!" He charges toward me again, but I hold up my hands, and threads of power shoot towards my palms. Flames immediately light them up and shoot out toward the man.

The man screams fill the entire hut, his entire body engulfed in flames, making him blend in with the room around him.

This is my only chance to leave, before it's too late. I need to go now!

Making sure I find the window again, I hop over the

side and land on my hands and knees. Inhaling fresh air, I cough as my lungs are full of thick smoke, and my entire body buzzes from the adrenaline coursing through my veins. I need to find Delilah. I stand back up and brace myself with the sudden surroundings. The sting in my cheek comes back to me, and I immediately hold my face, trying not to think about how big the cut is or how much blood I have already lost. The warmth fills my hand, and the wet blood starts dripping down and in between my fingers. The pain kicks into overdrive, starting from my ear to my neck.

Fuck!

I know this can't be good, and there isn't anything I can do right now to stop the bleeding. That is the least of my worries right now.

I need to find Delilah and get her home. I need to know if Daisy made it back to Mary... I know my wife will be worried sick for Delilah and myself.

Balancing myself on my feet, I rip apart the bottom of my shirt and tie it around my head, sort of similar to a bandana. I must try something to hopefully get the bleeding to stop... or at least to control it. It's at an awkward angle to wrap the makeshift bandage, but it'll have to do. I don't hesitate any long, I take off running down the path I told Delilah to take, I look left and right in every shadow, every corner, in the hopes of spotting her, but I don't.

I come up empty.

There is no one around.

Pure silence.

Where is she?

I take the path to the open road, leading to our home.

"Daddy!" I see a figure in the moonlight running towards me.

There she is - my baby girl.

"Delilah!" I make my legs pick up the speed and race to cover the distance between us.

I swoop her into my arms, just like I did when she was my little girl.

"Oh, honey, I'm so glad you're safe." Swirling her around twice, the pure joy I have in my heart is overwhelming. Knowing she is safe, she is with me. I can't express in words how grateful I am she is here. Here with me, right now.

Placing her back on her feet. I steady myself. My hand shoots to my face, and I wince from the pain.

"You're hurt." She notices the bandage on my face. It's probably soaked through; not much I can do about that right now.

"I'm okay; you don't need to worry about me. Are you okay?" Doing a proper scan of her body, looking her up and down... head to toe, making sure to check to see if there are any blood spots on her clothes.

"I'm okay, they didn't hurt me."

"But I found your blood."

"That wasn't mine," A small smile spreads on her lips.

That's my girl.

"Do I want to know?" I ask her.

"No, can we please go home now?" I nod, I take her hand in mine, and we follow the path leading to our home.

Deep down, in my gut, I know they will be back. They won't stop until someone pays, but this time, I will be ready for them.

Chapter Twelve

Arthur

After Mary's greeting, I thought she was going to kiss Delilah to death. I'm sad I missed the reunion with Mary and Daisy as well, but I'm sure it would have gone the same way as I'm seeing it now.

"Thank you, Arthur." Mary grabs my hand and squeezes it. The smile in her eyes, shows me the exact emotion I knew she'd have. Gratitude, love and relief.

Our girls are home and safe.

Then the realization kicks in. My face.

"Arthur! You're hurt!" Mary takes a step toward me, still holding onto my hand.

"It's nothing, go take care of the girls." I pull my free from her grasp.

She nods before walking off with Delilah and Daisy in tow.

Mary will take care of the girls, and I need to clean my cut before my wife can really pay attention to me. Taking the couple of steps to the makeshift bathroom, to the right of the hut, I step inside and notice a bowl full of water sitting under the mirror on the wall. Bracing myself for the inevitable pain, I unwrap the bandage from my face and see the bloody, deep cut lining my cheek. It's not as gruesome as I thought it would be, but it will surely leave a scar.

'You should be proud, I know I am.' Flyran's voice filters through my thoughts.

Taking a fresh cloth, I begin to clean the cut when I say, "How can I be? I killed people today." Saying the words out loud, but quietly as I can, so Mary and the girls don't hear. I haven't quite figured out how to talk back to him within my mind.

'You can channel it; you must focus and follow our connection.' He answers me. Sounds easy enough.

Closing my eyes, I focus on the gold strand of magic - floating around in my mind. I follow it, and it leads me straight to a door. I reach out to turn the handle and ....

'BE CAREFUL.' Flyran's alerted voice is so loud. It rattles my mind completely.

I turn the handle with care this time, and creek the door open just the slightest... and there, standing in a field of wildflowers, is Flyran.

'Well done, Great One.'

Stepping through the door and making sure I'm closing it behind me. It seems silly to close a door in my mind, but instinct took over, and I shut it anyway.

'This place is incredible, and it's been here the entire time?' I ask him, channelling the magic through my mind this time.

'Yes, you just needed time to get here.' He sounds so proud of me.

'That's because I am. None of my kind have bonded before, I am the first, and it's wonderful

to witness what potential your kind can do with a boost in magic.'

'Are you always in my thoughts?'

'I'm not in your thoughts exactly… I… hover.'

'Is there a way to block you out?' Closing the distance between us, I sit cross-legged next to him in the grass. He is so huge. I've never really taken him in until now. His feathers are brown with white tips. His black beak is pointy and sharp. His paws have white feathers on top, and his nails are a dull yellow. His brown wings are tucked to his sides, ready to take flight at any notice.

"We aren't really here…" I knew that sounded crazy the second it left my lips.

'No, to your surprise you are now walking to your apple fields.' I blink back the surprise. That can't be right. I am in the bathroom attending to my cut wound.

'I, on the other hand, am relaxing on my island.'

"How do I make this stop?"

"Just like how you started this communication, you just need to do it in reverse." I blink back the fog from my brain.

Thinking back to the connection I walked toward before and retracing my steps.

There, the door. I open it wide and blink back the night sky, the moonlight leading my way to the tree line.

I'm back to my present self.

I can't believe I can communicate with Flyran now. It'll make asking him questions easier, or when I need to talk to him.

The realization is starting to set in, that I have the ability to control three elemental powers.

This is so surreal.

FLYRAN - GRIFFIN

"You're not toying with your charge, are you?" Ameria stalks toward me.

"I wouldn't call toying..." I respond back. Her scaled tail flicks left to right. It's her annoying trait. I've picked up on a few of her tells over the years.

'Seems to me you are." She huffs a puff of hot, steamy smoke in my direction.

'He's just learnt he can harness three elements, control them is a different story. This is a big deal for him.' I never thought an elemental could do that but he's proving me wrong.

"Your report from when you observed him?" She asks me, curiosity in her eyes.

"Nothing, very interesting creature. Doing the mundane tasks. He's quite boring, if I'm being honest... Are you sure he is the first of his kind?'

'Strange, and why do you ask?' She asks me, stopping in her tracks.

'Well, it feels different to me, like something is off, and you have been around a lot longer than any of us... I'm sure you would have seen something like this.'

'I have not. The magic now is changing, and I can't foresee what it will become.' She walks away from me. Leaving me with more questions than I had to begin with.

I wonder if the others can feel the shift in magic just as Ameria and I can. Will they have bonds with the elemental as well?

Can we create a link with more than one?

Chloe O'Connor

I wish I had more answers to the questions I seek.

Chapter Thirteen

Ameria - Dragon

The magic in the realm is shifting. It hasn't had a shift, not even in the slightest, since the time it was created, and that was well over ten thousand years ago. I am the only creature alive with a lineage that's seen the beginning of time. There have been stories passed down to me that talk about the magic being created, the magic growing and evolving.

Would that make me the anchor of it?

I would say yes and no.

I'm tied to magic, but I'm not the creator of magic. It's a part of me; I am the elder of the others and the final decision maker. It's a lot of weight to carry, but I know my time in the realm will soon be over and the next dragon will descend to take my place as elder.

For now, something is brewing in the Fae lands. I can't put my claw on it, but there's a shift in the magic. I must make sure the Guardians are prepared for whatever we are about to get thrown. However, Flyran has already felt that shift. He's now bonded to a Fae, an elemental. I can't believe it.

Never in my wildest dreams did I think it was possible to share the same magic thread with other beings outside of the Guardianship.

Flyran has proven to me, and soon to the others that it is possible.

Will we understand the risks that are associated with it? No.

Can we choose who we bond to? Or does it happen by nature?

The balance of it all, the shift in good and evil. That's something we need to keep a close eye on.

The next high council meeting is soon, and I must bring this topic up to them carefully. To prepare them, because it might, in fact happen to them as well. I can't leave them blindsided. I don't know how Flyran dealt with this on his own. Sure, he told me in the end, but he had to deal with the shift on his own. He has proven his strength, time and time again. I commend him for that.

I still can't shake the feeling of the shift in the magic. Have I felt something like this before?

No.

Can I already predict that the harmony of the lands is starting to turn from peaceful to hatred and destruction?

Yes.

There is no way of stopping it; we must let it run its course, for how many years will this take? That I'm unsure of.

"Ameria, it is time," Flyran's voice filters through to my mind.

We can communicate with one another through our minds; that is a formed connection we all share.

And it seems it's passed down to the elementals as well.

I'm still in awe when I see all the giant guardians

standing around a boulder-shaped table, patiently waiting for me to enter the cave. The weather outside is harsh, and being inside is the protection we need against the pouring rain, lightning and damaging winds. It looks like we must ride it out. Those of us with wings can't risk flying out in that. I won't allow for that kind of stupidity.

"What are we doing here, Ameria?" Aoura mumbles from the corner. Ouroboros doesn't do well in crowds even though we are all basically family.

"Yeah! Couldn't have this waiting until the rain stops!" Philnox chimes in. The phoenix isn't pleased with rain; they usually remain inside their own cave because it weakens their power if they are caught in rain. I guess none of the guardians leave their cave unless it's something that brings them joy or our council meetings.

"No!" I demand.

He huffs a steam of smoke, clearly frustrated nothing I can do about that right now.

"I've called you all here because there's been a shift in the magic. I'm not sure if you have felt something and haven't said anything, or have chosen to ignore it, but now that you are all here. We have something serious to discuss, and no, it couldn't have waited, and no, we couldn't have talked via telepathically. This needed to be had in the flesh." I take in each guardian, their blank expressions. Okay, if that's how you want to play this game. Let's get on with it then.

"Flyran has bonded to an elemental Fae. Something we have never seen or heard of happening before."

"What are you talking about? I haven't felt anything." Seran, the Sea Serpent, responds.

"I know this may come as a shock, it was to Flyran and me, but we have come to terms with it. We wanted you all to know that there may come a time when you'll bond with an elemental. We don't know what the lengths of sharing a bond will do."

"What does it feel like?" The question was directed to Flyran.

"It's like the bridge connection to our magic, but there's another gateway. You can communicate with them, just like we do, and they can harness our power. It's strange but also thrilling knowing I can communicate with them."

They all look amongst themselves and murmur their surprise.

"Do we wait for the connection to form, or do we choose an elemental?" Philox asks me. I'm not sure how to answer that. I have also asked this question to myself and have come up empty.

"I think it's best we wait. Flyran didn't seek out the elemental ; the bond just... happened." They all nod their agreement.

"Are there any other questions?" I ask the group, taking them in one by one.

"No." they say in unison.

"Alright, meeting dismissed." They all start to slither, walk, or fly out of the cave. Thankfully it had stopped raining.

"Flyran, wait," I call after the Griffin.

"Yeah?"

"Let's go take a visit to your elemental Fae. I want to meet him in the flesh. I want to get a good reading on him, maybe if he's not worthy of the bond, I can burn him on the spot."

"Surely not!" Flyran turns his whole body toward me.

"It's to keep the magical balance. I'll do anything to protect it. Now let's go."

Chapter Fourteen

Mary

"Arty," I call my husband's name, loud enough for the nearby villages to hear. Still, it's impossible as they are several miles away... so you can imagine just how loud I really had to call his name...

"Yes, my love." His voice sounding cool, calm and collected. I hear his footsteps coming closer to me.

"You need to come out here," I demand.

Finally, I hear his footsteps stop behind me, and now I shift my own feet from the nerves I'm feeling.

The sight before me is astonishing. Right in front of me are two enormous creatures. I am frozen with fear. I can only hear the thump, thump of my heartbeat in my ears.

These creatures should only be folklore, nothing that should be presented in reality, let alone right in front of me.

"Flyran what are you doing here!?" Arthur's voice is low, almost like an angry whisper.

Wait.

He said its name.

"Arthur!?" I turn around and face him. Not sure if that

was the best move with these giant creatures behind me. Creatures that shouldn't exist.

"Oh, but we do." The voice filters through my mind.

Spinning back around, my mouth wide open in shock.

"Did you just..." Almost comes out in a whisper.

"Close your mouth, Fae. It's impolite to stare." It's that voice again.

I turn to my husband again, "Where are the girls?" I don't want them to see these creatures and get scared, scarred for a lifetime, and then some.

"Collecting harvest, they should be gone for another hour or so." Good, I can't have them being here.

Turning back to face these creatures, squaring my shoulders. I must be strong here. Show them that they can't hurt us.

"What are you doing here?" I demand, staring at the largest one in front of me.

"We have come to see Arthur." The smallest one speaks through my mind.

"What do you need with him?" I reply. I don't let Arthur chime in. He will have enough time later to explain exactly what is happening, but right now I need to take charge.

"Not your concern, Fae." The largest one speaks again. I watch on as the smaller one turns to the larger one. Are they talking to each other?

Tilting my head to the side, I watch in admiration between the two. They are fascinating.

"Arthur, what are they?" I whisper as I feel his hand brace my back.

"The smallest one is Flyran, he is a Griffin. He's a lion and eagle." Taking in his strong four legs, holding up his enormous golden fur body, and his neckline is lined with stunning white feathers, and his golden-brown beak is sharp in the sunlight. His tail swishes from side to side, and his black and golden feathers encase his wings, which are tucked to his sides. I am in awe.

"The largest one is Ameria; she is a dragon." He doesn't need to elaborate. What in the guardian's name are they doing here ? She's the colour of midnight; her scales seem so smooth and shiny in the sunlight. A dagger-like shape at the end of her tail, moving every so often, her large black wings tucked in on either side of her body. I can barely see the faint scar over her right eye. She looks magnificent.

"I can't believe what I am seeing. Of course, you heard the myths and legends of them growing up, but to have them actually standing in front of you is completely insane." Arthur pats my shoulder in reassurance.

"You get used to it, my love." Squeezing my shoulder, he lets go and takes a step forward.

"I don't mean to interrupt, but my girls will be returning shortly, and I don't want them to see you both." It turns silent, and they both turn toward Arthur, watching as Ameria tilts her head... examining him.

"Very well." Ameria's voice sounds annoyed and bored at the same time.

"Why are you here?" I demand, my patience running a little dry.

"We wanted to check on Arthur."

"Check on him? For what? To make sure he hasn't gone crazy from the sightings of you. For what!" I can feel my temper rising.

"I want answers now!" I keep demanding. I want answers. I need them.

"Arthur, it's best coming from you." Flyran's voice filters through my mind.

"If she doesn't keep her temper in check, I'll bite off her head." Ameria directs that comment to Arthur, but she made sure I heard her.

Message received, making it crystal clear.

I turn to face Arthur once more, hoping he'd look me in the eye and confess whatever is eating at him. It's been this big kept secret for months. I thought he would come out and tell me already, like he normally would, but this time he has kept it to himself.

He takes a step closer, closing the space between us. He reaches down and takes my hands in his.

"We are born Water Fae. You, me and Delilah. But I have also been granted the power of Fire and Air." Did I just hear him correctly?

Inherited powers. Been gifted more elemental gifts.

"I don't understand. That's unheard of."

"It is, but something is shifting in the realm, and Arthur seemed impacted by it. He's also bonded to Flyran, where he can communicate with him, draw on the link between them to gain more power, and we have not tested how far this bond will go. Does it last through death?" My shock rushes through my entire body.

Death!

"You will not be trying that!"

"We aren't going to test any theories, we don't want to risk breaking the bond, but you must know that having knowledge about my powers is extremely dangerous. We must be extra careful around the villages. They know something is going on. It's for the protection of you and the girls."

"Fine, but they," I say, pointing to the Griffin and Dragon, "need to leave."

"Suits us. " The dragon nods and takes flight in a split second. The Griffin hesitates for a second before following the dragon.

"What have you done?" I ask Arthur, before turning away from him to go back inside.

Chapter Fifteen

Ameria -Dragon

"Did you have to be such a bitch?" Flyran connects to my mind, asking me mid-flight on the return home.

"I was no such thing." I reply.

"You were. Admit it."

I was only harsh toward the fae beings. That female one had quite the attitude. If it wasn't for Flyran, I would have burned her alive.

I'm not used to that kind of interaction, dealing with the smaller, lesser beings.

"I don't have to do such a thing."

"I think it's best if I interact with the fae's from now on. Let's keep you at a distance..." He trails off.

"Fine but don't blame me if they decide to capture you and kill you for your skin." I growl.

"I can handle myself!" He shoots back.

"If you say so, Flyran..." Trying to gather my thoughts for what I'm about to say next.

"Yeah?"

"Something big is coming, and I think we need to be

prepared... I can feel it." There is something in the air I'm starting to get really worried about, I just can't explain it.

"Are we heading to the council?"

"Yes." We need to explain what's happened further.

The rest of the flight was silent besides the wind in the air and the coolness breeze against my wings.

I have felt the shift in magic coming for a while now. I didn't want to admit out loud to Flyran. He is my closest companion, and to admit defeat is something I will never do. I am their leader; I must remain strong and smart about what's about to happen.

Walking along the cold rubble floor toward the council is never daunting. For some reason, I enjoy being their leader, the person they look up to. Someone who will take charge and make the tough decisions. Today, though... I wish I'd get burnt alive.

The deep gut feeling is something that hasn't gone away since Flyran bonded with that fae.

"What's the meaning for this?" Samundra asked impatiently.

Flyran and I thought you deserved to know that we met with the fae beings. I wanted to meet them for myself, to see if they are a risk to *our* kind."

"And?" Rymaro urges me to continue.

"They are safe... for now. Maybe a little bit of an attitude but I applaud them for their bravery for speaking to me in that manner."

"Oh, so you admit that now?" Flyran chuckles beside me.

I whip him with my tail. The others don't need to know that.

"What are we going to do now?" Samundra asks.

"Wait and see. I know it's not the answer you want to hear but right now Flyran has a charge... Arthur and that's going to be his number one priority. We don't know how bonded they are, right down to the extent of wounds, drawing of power or death."

Silence.

They don't understand the extent of having a bonded fae really is.

I wish I could tell me everything that has been passed down to me, our ancestors, the knowledge but it's never been my decision.

This....

This is all new and I must learn how to handle it.

"Okay," they all say in unison.

Chapter Sixteen

Arthur

That meeting could have gone better, so much better, and I wish they would have given me some warning instead of just showing up at my hut. A part of me wishes I told Mary before Flyran made himself known to her, but I didn't and couldn't form the right words. I know this day will haunt me for the rest of my life. How can I face Mary now and make things right with her? There are no words - nothing to make this situation better. What's done is done.

I follow Mary's footsteps; I need to find her and explain it from my perspective. I quickly rack my brain to come up with something, anything, to say to her.

"Mary?" I call out for her.

"In here." Her voice comes from the right of our hut. Our bedroom.

This isn't good. She only hides in there when she wants to be alone. Now wouldn't be any different, if not worse, right now.

Turning the corner, I brace for her wrath.

"Mary..."

"Arthur, I don't know what you are right now. Stay away from them... from us... until I can think."

"Mary... my love." I kneel in front of her, taking in her soft feature, the way her smile lines crinkle near her eyes. Years and years of laughter cause them, or the way her forehead wrinkles with anger, or how tiny she tends to make herself when she wants to be left alone. There isn't anything I can do to make this right, but I can try. I start by taking her hands in mine. I search her eyes, and I'm immediately taken back to the first moment I saw her.

She was so young, beautiful, and vibrant. The second my eyes landed on her, I knew I wanted her to be my wife.

"Can we please talk about this?"

"Sure, this conversation will end up like all the rest... You will do all the talking, and then I'll forgive you... But not this time Arthur. I can't believe you've kept this secret from me, a very important one!! Life-changing one might I add." She pulls her hands from mine and stands up- steps around and away from me. I follow suit.

"Mary, please," I beg her.

"No, Arthur. I need space. I need time."

"For how long?" Taking a step closer.

"As long as it takes, I can't be near you right now. This has truly hurt me, hurt me deep into my core, Arthur. You must understand that. This isn't going to be an easy fix between us. I love you, but I can't forgive you. Not right now at least. Please go find the girls; you will need to tell them as well. It'll keep them safer if they know the truth." She takes another look at me and points to the doorway of our bedroom. She wants to be left alone, and that's exactly what I'll give her. I know she needs this time to cool down, to think things through, and process exactly what she just encountered. I will give that to her.

She is the love of my life.

* * *

It's been two hours since I spoke to the girls about the mythical guardians being real. The girls took it better than Mary; they were excited and wanted to meet them. I told them maybe one day. But for now, they need to remain secret, and of course, I don't control them, so it'll have to be on their terms.

The walk back to our hut was in such high spirits, if Mary saw the girls excited and happy about the news, maybe Mary could get on board with it as well. Instead, I see dark grey and black smoke filling the air towards our hut. I inhale a sharp breath. That's where our hut is.

No.

No.

"Stay here!" I yell at the girls and take off sprinting in the direction of the smoke.

The wind is thrashing in my face as I draw closer to the hut. Getting closer, I see large red and orange flames dance around the outside of the hut, massive flames consuming the barn next to it.

No.

No.

No.

This can't be happening.

"Mary!" I call my wife's name.

No answer.

Silence.

"MARY!" I yell louder. Hoping she can somehow hear me above the wisps of burning wood and flame shooting into the sky.

But the silence is deafening.

Nothing.

All I hear is the crackling of the fire. Destroying everything in its path.

I need to stop it. I must stop it.

The connection to my power is stronger than ever before. I channel the power link to Flyran and pull everything within me, summoning the magic within me, I call to air. I need it to squish the flames to the ground, concealing it to a tiny box. Letting nothing inside or letting anything escape it. There needs to be no oxygen feeding the fire; it goes out.

The air hisses, and in a split second, the fire is out. Leaving a shattered and blackened hut in its wake.

I still don't see Mary anywhere.

"Mary!" I call out, running around both sides of the hut. Maybe she is hiding somewhere and is too frightened to leave her safety spot.

Silence.

There is only one place I'm scared to my bones in checking; I need to step inside the ash-ridden hut. I send a silent prayer up to the Guardians that I don't find Mary inside. Looking around the once standing kitchen and seeing the only silver pot remaining gives me a chill down my spine.

I know I left Mary in our bedroom before I went to the girls. I'm hoping she left to get help from one of our nearby neighbours.

Hesitation hits, I can't bring myself to step inside our bedroom.

I know once I step inside, there is no turning back.

Scanning the room, I see nothing unusual... taking another step inside the room...

There... in the corner near the top end of our bed, is something.

I sink to my knees.

A figure of a body.

A body that once belonged to my wife sits on the floor. The fire hadn't started long ago, so you could see exactly what happened to her.

Crawling on my hands and knees to her, I cradle her burnt body in mine. Seeing that she was bound by her wrists and ankles. Keeping her tied in this exact spot when the fire started.

"Oh, Mary... my sweet Mary... my love. What have they done to you?"

Hot, wet tears slide down my cheeks as I close my eyes and picture the last conversation we had.

"I'm so sorry." I sob into the side of her head.

"I should have been here; I should have stayed; I could have saved you." Emotion takes over every fibre of my being. My sweet Mary, she's gone.

'There isn't anything you can do now, Great One.' Flyran's voice filters through the fog in my head.

'Think of the little ones.' He reminds me of my daughter and niece who are yet to walk to the hut. They can't see Mary like this.

They can't.

Slowly, I lay her body to the ground, wishing things were different. Willing the ache in my chest to go away. I know I must be brave when I see the two girls.

Trying to gather all the courage I can muster to try to explain to them what has just happened...

Chapter Seventeen

Mary

I don't know how I'm ever going to forgive Arthur about the secret he's been keeping. This is a huge secret to hide and it's the fact that he didn't feel the need to tell me speaks volumes.

Gaining two extra elemental powers is one thing, but to be bonded to a mythical creature that has only ever been told in folklore is another. I can't imagine what the weight of this burden has done to Arthur and for him to think he didn't need to or want to share this with me is heartbreaking. I wouldn't have thought anything less of him, I thought he would have known that. We have always been honest with each other, to never hide anything from one another.

That's why I'm finding this to be so hard. He's my best friend, and now I don't know who he is.

Arthur has just left the hut and taken the girls away. I'm sure it's time for him to tell them, fill them in on what's been happening, but I am hoping he's filtering out a lot of things they don't need to know.

I settle on our bed, head resting against the soft pillow and looking up to the ceiling.

How can I forgive him?

How can we move forward after this?

What happens when the villagers find out?

There are so many questions I just wish I had the answers to.

"It doesn't look like anyone's home, let's get out of here!" Startled awake, I hear voices outside the hut. I don't dare to move. I don't dare make a sound.

"Let's just check inside..." Another man's voice sounds closer than the first.

"I don't think that's a good idea." The first man replies.

"Come on, we have come this far. We can't just turn back now."

"Fine but let's be quick about it."

I hear the front door of the hut open and close quietly. There's not a sound I can hear besides my own breathing. The footsteps start to get closer and closer to the bedroom door. Sitting up quickly, I scan the bedroom and curse.

There isn't anywhere I can hide in here.

I don't have anything of value to offer them if they are here to rob the place. I really wish Arthur was here.

The door handle of the bedroom door slowly turns. My heart is beating so loud in my ears, that's the only thing I can focus on.

Boom, boom, boom. My heart pounding, faster and faster.

"What do we have here?" A man steps inside the room and locks eyes with me.

"You must leave, my husband will be home any minute and I don't think you want to piss him off." I tilt my head up, showing the invisible courage, I have.

"Oh, we are counting on it." The other man says, stepping inside the room.

An internal shiver runs down my spine. these men mean trouble and now I really wish I didn't send Arthur away... at least the girls aren't here.

"I don't want to wait any longer." The smaller of the two comments.

"Okay, she will have to do," The tallest one steps forward and produces rope.

My eyes go wide at the site.

"No, no, no. Please, don't do this." moving my body away from the men, but it's cut short when my back hits the wall behind me.

Fuck.

"There is nowhere to run, nowhere to hide. We have you now." The men close the distance and grab me by the ankles.

I try to kick my legs free but it's no use. They are too strong for me.

Tying my feet together with the rope I saw earlier, they throw me to the floor beside the bed, bound my wrists.

"Any last words?" The tallest man says to me,

"You will get what's coming to you." I spit the words out.

"Gage her." The other man pulls cloth from his pocket and shoves it in my mouth.

"Stew on these words Mary... Arthur was the one who is going to kill you, not us." With those last words said, the shortest man closes his hands together and fire erupts from them.

He points to the ground and fire leaps down and starts spreading online the floor, the walls and furniture of the bedroom.

I am going to die here.

Chapter Eighteen

Arthur

Telling the girls Mary died has been the hardest thing for me. Watching my daughter fall to her knees in pure heartbreak wasn't something I'd ever want to witness in my lifetime. Daisy has been the only strong one between the three of us. Silent but so strong in her presence.

Grief is no stranger to her.

I couldn't bring myself to let the girls inside and see Mary for themselves. I know it'll haunt them for the rest of their lives. I know it will haunt mine. Instead, I told them to wait outside and think of Mary in the loving and sweetest memories they could.

Walking into the barn, the smell of smoke stings my nose, and the emptiness it all feels. Luckily only half of the barn was affected by the fire. Grabbing spare blankets, I keep aside for the horse, I spot the furthest corner away from the hut and check the flooring.

The hay is clean, no burnt patches. Lying the blankets down for the girls, I call them in.

"Delilah, Daisy."

Slow footsteps get louder and louder.

"You can't expect us to sleep here!" Delilah protests.

"My sweet daughter," Standing up on my feet, closing the distance between us. "There really isn't any other option except outside in the Elements."

"It'll be okay." Daisy softly speaks.

"Fine." She huffs and kneels and rests on the soft blankets I laid out.

"I am going to the hut over the hill. Please don't leave the barn, I won't be gone long." I bend over and kiss both girls on the head.

Walking away, but before exiting the barn, I turn around.

"I mean it, no leaving the barn." I warn both the girls. They don't say anything, they don't move. They're just frozen in shock still.

I don't blame them.

An hour has passed since I sent word to my brother-in-law to come collect Daisy. I am hoping he is well and on the mend since his wife's death. I can now understand how grief took this man's soul and purpose to function, but I can also not understand how he can just leave Daisy. I would never do that to Delilah.

Both girls are asleep once in returned. I knew it wouldn't be long. Both emotional and physically exhausted. I know my body is due to give out but I don't have the time to rest. There is so much to be done.

"Daisy?" A man's voice echoes the fields outside.

I meet him in the doorway of the barn.

"Petrye."

"Arthur, is that you?" He steps into view.

My brother-in-law is now standing in front of me, looking very well, since the last time I saw him. He looks much better, fitted clothes, washed and healthier.

The time away from his daughter must have been a wakeup call.

"It's me." He holds out his hand for a shake and I take it. He pulls me in tighter for a hug.

"I am so sorry about Mary. I came as soon as I received word."

"Thank you, I appreciate it." Taking a step back and out of his embrace.

"Where's Daisy?" He asks.

"Asleep, in the back corner."

"Thank you." He steps around me and heads toward the sleeping girls.

"You came in a decent time, not far from here?" I ask him. There is no way he would have made it this quick if he was living near Earth boundary like he used to.

"No, I moved to be closer to Daisy, for when the day she needed me again."

"She's needed you since the day you dropped her off at my doorstep. Don't put that blame back on her, that was your fault, and you only have yourself to blame."

He stops walking and turns back around to face me. Tension rising in the air around us.

"You're right, I let the grief of my dead wife consume my entire being, I'm sure you would know that feeling..." He trials off.

Is he being serious right now?

"Yes, the grief of losing Mary is there but I would never abandon my daughter because of it. I will only get stronger because of her." There are a time and place for this conversation and right now is not it.

"Daddy?" Daisy's sleepy voice silences everything in the hut.

"Yes, my baby." Petrye closes the distance between him and his daughter, embracing her in his arms.

"I have missed you so much."

"I have missed you more, are you here to take me home?" She asks.

"I am baby girl, I am." He lets her go.

"Uncle!" Delilah rushes out and hugs him hello.

"It's good to see you, Delilah." He returns her hug.

"Well, I would love to stay but it's late and I want to get Daisy home." Petrye takes hold of his daughter's hand.

"Let me say goodbye to Delilah." She takes her hand out of his and quickly embraces Delilah.

"I will miss you."

"I will miss you too, cousin." Delilah whispers into Daisy's hair.

Seeing the girls say goodbye to each other tore another piece away from my heart. I can't deal with any more loss. I just won't.

Grief has its own language.

Chapter Nineteen

Arthur

Mary's funeral is today. We only lost her yesterday.

Delilah and I decided to put her to rest as soon as possible so her spirit has a better chance to roam the afterlife in peace.

"I can't do this; I can't say goodbye to mum. I just won't." Delilah crosses her arms over her chest. We stop in the middle of the field, on our way to the resting ground for Mary. I turn to my daughter; her cheeks were wet from the free-flowing tears.

"My sweet girl, I know this must be the most impossible task right now, and I wish I could take that pain away from you, but this is how your mother wanted it. She wanted her family surrounded by each other and to remember all the great things she accomplished in her life... you." I softly grab her by both arms and pull her into me. Wrapping my arms around her tightly, I let her small frame comfort me, just this once. It should be the other way around, me comforting her, but right now I just can't. I've lost the love of my life, the mother of our daughter. My heart aches for her, for me, and the possible future we would have had. Our time together was cut short, and I will never forgive myself. Not being there for her, not saving her when I know I could have. It will haunt me until my last dying breath. I will count down the seconds until we are united again. I don't get to see her grow old beside me. I don't get to see her smile one last time, hear her laugh beside me, or watch my daughter talk to her mother.

A daughter always needs their mother.

I don't wish this feeling on anyone... but maybe to those who killed my wife - tortured her. The heat in my body starts to rise.

'*Easy.*' Flyrans' voice echoes in my mind.

I try to block him out. I can't have him jumping into my thoughts today, of all days. Today is a day I need for myself and my daughter.

The spot we've chosen for Mary is in a Daffodil field; those were her favourite flowers. She once said that the brightness of the yellow always made her happy, even if she was having a shitty day.

Her words.

Flowers were always Mary's favourite. She joked about naming our Daughter Daffodil, and she said that although the flowers were beautiful, they were nothing compared to our daughter. There was no match.

I agreed.

So, we decided on Delilah, which was the perfect match for our daughter.

The walk to the grave was still. There was no wind; it was just pure silence. It's almost like the earth knows a tragedy happened, and is grieving, too. I take comfort in that, only just a little bit.

The freshly dug-up ground was an indication of exactly where Mary would rest. My hands, shaky from spending most of the night digging up the hard, frozen ground. The frost set in overnight and made it nearly impossible to dig up, but Flyran offered to help, and I accepted.

Honestly, I don't know what I would do without him. He has been an incredible rock for me, the support I have needed.

Seeing the grave in the daylight has hit me to my core. My chest is beginning to grow tight, my heartbeat thumping in my ears.

I can't do this. I can't say goodbye to the love of my life. How can she not be here anymore? I sink to my knees, the pain in my chest is becoming unbearable.

"Father! Father, are you okay?" Delilah rushes to my side, holding onto my arm.

"I'm okay, my sweet... baby girl." Inhaling deep breaths in between speaking. Trying to get my breath back, it's all-consuming.

Guilt.

She shouldn't have to be taking care of me right now; I must remain the strong one, for the both of us.

My thoughts won't stop, though, the guilt I feel.

How is this fair!

It should be me in the ground; they wanted me! Not her!

Reflecting on our last conversation and how mad she was with me, I wish I had of stayed to fix it and not left her, alone.

I wish I had of told her the truth about my growing powers.

I would give them up in a heartbeat if I knew I could bring Mary back. No questions asked. I wish I could trade spots with her, let her live with Delilah, grow old, and experience the world again. Why me? Why do I have to continue, and Mary is the one who had to leave this land?

A daughter needs her mother.

'It was her time...' Flyran's voice is merely a whisper in my mind. I have tried so hard to block him out. I know he helped with Mary, but I need all my thoughts today. I just want one day without him invading my mind - just one.

Instead of more words filtering through my mind, I feel the power humming in my veins, knowing he is instantly here, controlling my power, helping me... guiding me.

Crawling the two feet in front of me to make it to the edge of the overturned dirt. I knew burying her before the kids woke up was the best idea. I didn't want them to see her like that. The way her entire body was black, burned. Barely any skin covering her bones, the way her body was manipulated, tied, and I knew deep inside that she died in pain. That she suffered, and I wasn't there to help her. To save her.

"Oh, Mary." I drop my head to the dirt. Tears escaping my eyes, warming my cheeks, and dripping to the dirt beneath my hands.

"I am so sorry I wasn't there; I am so sorry I couldn't save you. Oh, my wife." The tears are coming harder now; my entire body is shaking with the heartache. The pain in my chest was vibrating, the tightness, and I knew in that moment I wanted to be beside her. I can't move on and leave her here... alone.

"Daddy." My daughter's voice croaks on my name. She drops down beside me, bracing myself on my knees, I pull my daughter into me. I cradle her like I did when she was a child. A tiny little girl who cried over a scrapped knee, something I could fix back then, but now. This heartache I will never be able to fix, nothing I can do to replace this broken heart for her. The only thing that can replace Delilah and my complete heartbreak is bringing Mary back from the dead, but we know that's impossible.

Our Mary is gone... forever.

"I'm so sorry." I rock her, saying sorry to both of them. To Mary whom I couldn't save, and to our daughter for losing her mother.

"I'm so sorry."

"I'm so sorry."

"I'm so sorry." Whispering the words over and over.

Chapter Twenty

Arthur

An hour had passed of just Delilah and me crying, telling stories about our Mary, only the good times that we spent together, which was a lot. Mary never had a bad day and if she did, it wouldn't last long. She was the most forgiving woman in this realm. She didn't deserve that death; she didn't deserve to be taken from us. I will murder those who took her away from us.

"Sorry to interrupt this reunion." The deep, croaky male voice comes from behind us.

An immediate chill runs down my spine. This isn't good. I slowly reach for Delilah's hand.

"You need to run, run as fast as you can." I squeeze it.

I close my eyes for a split second, drawing all the strength and power from Flyran.

This ends now.

I open the door to Flyran and quickly send him a message. I need him. ***'Coming!'*** He tells me.

"Now!" I yell.

Standing up, I shield Delilah running away with my body. My body will always be used as a shield to protect her. I couldn't save Mary, but I will die trying to save my daughter.

"What are you doing here? Haven't you done enough?" My voice is level, steady. No trace of fear or emotion. I will not back down. These men killed my wife, my love.

"We don't think so." He chuckles and looks around at his men. I follow his line of sight and count them; there are maybe eight men in total.

Easy.

"You couldn't let a family grieve a murdered family member in peace?" I taunt. Hoping to catch him off guard and admit that he killed my wife. The only woman I have ever truly loved and will always be the love of my life.

"There is no peace for you, monster." He takes a step forward and before he can think of his last thought my power is vibrating with such force, it's beckoning to be released, and I let it.

I turn my hands upward and flick my fingers out. Letting the fire shoot from my palms, inviting these bastards to take a step closer.

"Come on now, don't be shy. I promise I don't bite..." I smile, a wicked smile. There is no holding back.

"Get him." He yells at his men, and they all take off sprinting in my direction.

"Let's play." I laugh into the air. I will die trying today to avenge my wife's murderer.

The power within me sends the flame in my palms to shoot higher, and the heat warms my face.

"This is for Mary!" I yell and face my palms to the first two men on my left. The flame flicks and swims through the air in their direction.

I don't bother looking; I can tell I've hit my mark by the

sudden screams I hear. The immediate painful sounds tell me I've hit my target. Perfect.

I know they should be dead in a matter of seconds. The heat of the flames alone will be melting their skin off their bones. A quick death. Unlike Mary, who suffered.

I turn to my right, and another three men are too close for comfort.

I quickly call the air power within me to the forefront of my mind, and I summon a mini tornado. The sky above changes color, from bright cloudless blue to a dark, nasty, black-covered sky. The wind picks up so fast, it's terrifying. I watch as a spiral comes down from the sky. It's the tornado I summoned.

Using my mind, I direct the tornado to take the three men who are the closest to me and discard them far away from this exact spot. I know the impact with the ground again would kill them instantly. I wish I could take my time killing these men, but I know the threat they pose is far greater with Delilah in the fields somewhere.

"Stop him!" The ringleader cries out; he is panicking now. He knows I've got him. He has nowhere to go, and there are no rookies to help take me out. Nothing.

Revenge is so sweet on my tongue.

The last two men are coming at me from behind. I whirl around in time to face them, a wicked smile playing on my lips. I've been saving this last power trick just for one of them, but if I can kill both at the same time - bonus points for me.

"Get him, you idiots! Just like you got his wife." His words, acid on my tongue.

I see red.

Anger. Rage. Guilt.

It's all simmering to the top, and I summon water. I

imagine the water running through their bodies, using what water they have inside to smother them from the inside out. I will not let them breathe in the air surrounding them, drowning them and making sure they suffer.

Slowly.

Painfully.

They sink to their knees, holding their throats. No words escaping, nothing.

Just silence.

I know they can't do anything more than to lie there and wither away...

Turning around, I focus my entire attention on the ringleader.

"Considered how you'd like to die... from the monster?" I ask him. Taunting him.

Suddenly, I see Mary's face in my mind.

Her beautiful smile, the small wrinkles framing her face and eyes. The way she would touch my cheek in a loving way, her warmth of her hand and breath against my skin.

"Mary?" I ask out loud to no one and to everyone who is here.

Blinking back the fresh tears, I regain my focus, and it's now locked back onto the ringleader.

His entire body shivers; the fear is shining through his eyes. I've got him. There is no escaping me now. I will kill every single man who is a threat to me or my daughter. You have my word.

"No, please." He takes a step backward. His hands are up and out in front of him.

He's begging.

How cute.

"Now, now. Mary didn't have a fighting chance, it's

rude to let you have the same courtesy." I take two steps closer to him.

THUD.

Flyran lands right behind the ringleader.

THUD.

Flyran takes a single step closer to the ringleader.

"Impeccable timing, my friend," I call out to him.

'Always.' I can almost hear the smirk in his voice.

The ringleader turns around and sees Flyran, the Mythical Griffin, standing there, wings spread wide, his head low and, his beak glistening in the sun.

"Wha... wha..." he stutters. "What are you?" He asks, taking in Flyrans at full height.

"He's a Griffin, you know... the one who created a monster," I smirk, a hint of a laugh behind my words.

"Please!" He begs, and before he can get his next words out, Flyran takes one step forward and his beak aims for his throat. Puncturing a hole dead centre. The ringleader bleeds out in seconds.

I stand there, shocked, but also relieved.

'It had to be done.' Flyran flaps his wings, not apologetic in the slightest.

"Thank you." Turning around full circle, I take in the sight before me.

Men, dead on the ground surrounding Mary's grave.

She hated violence.

I wish it hadn't had to come to this, but it had to be done.

Bowing my head, "I'm sorry, my love."

With one fluid motion of my hand, flames consume the dead bodies, and they are gone in seconds.

Leaving no trace of them at all.

"Dad." My daughter's voice breaks through all the chaos surrounding me.

Delilah! I run toward her voice and meet her just atop the hill, close to Mary's grave. I quickly wrap her in my arms, lifting her off the ground and snuggling into her.

"It's okay, sweet girl, they are gone," I whisper into her ear.

"Looks like we missed one hell of a party." A male's voice says over Delilah's shoulder. I let go of my daughter and see my brother-in-law and niece standing not too far away.

"What are you doing here?" I ask

"Daisy wanted to say goodbye to Aunt Mary. I wasn't going to deny her that." I nod. Agreeing and grateful for the timing as well.

"Let's go." Letting go of Delilah, I take her hand instead, and we walk to the resting ground of Mary once more.

This time, we can say our final goodbye in peace.

Chapter Twenty-One

Arthur

'*You fought well fae.*' I know that voice, turning around I see Ameria stepping out of the shadows.

I step in front of my family. Shielding them with my body, I don't want anything to happen to them.

'**Fool, I am not going to harm them.**' Reading my thoughts. I thought only the bonded can do that.

'**I do not need to be bonded to break the shields down on anyone's mind I wish to invade. I am a dragon, the leader of the Mythical Creatures. I am power.**' She emphasis on the words power.

Got it.

Turning to Flyran, I have a burning question I need to ask.

"How did I manifest such power?" Tornadoes when I couldn't even get apples off a tree not that long ago.

'**Me. I helped manifest your power. Whatever willed your power into, I made it happen. You're too novice to create anything that powerful yet.**' Now that makes more sense and grateful that I had him to assist me.

"Thank you." I trail off. I have this gut feeling something is about to happen...

'It's time to go.' Flyran's voice filters through.

I knew this was coming. I can no longer stay here. There will be more ringleaders, more evil men trying to destroy me and my family, and I can't let that happen. Not when I have the choice to stop it and bring peace to these lands once more.

"I know," I murmur out loud. How can I say goodbye to my daughter? How can I leave her here?

'You must...' Flyran insists.

"My sweet daughter," I step toward her, reaching for her face, I cradle her cheek in the palm of my hand.

"I'm sorry. I wish I didn't have to do this, but I must leave. It's the only way to keep you and everyone here safe. They won't stop hunting me..." I trail off, I don't want to bring back Mary's death for her or the events that happened today.

"Why can't we go together?" Tears form at the corner of her eyes again, watching as one tear slowly escapes and leaves a wet trail down her cheek. I wipe it away.

"There is only room for one on Flyran, and I'm the one they want. You can live a peaceful life here with your cousin and uncle." I look up and nod to my brother-in-law. He was a hard man to track down, but once news reached him about Mary's death, he came as soon as he could for his daughter. Grateful he showed up last night and today.

'Now!' Flyran's voice is sounding very impatient.

I look toward Flyran, in the hopes I can have a final talk with Ameria, but she is nowhere to be seen.

'She has returned home. I am to take care of this situation.' Almost sounds like I an inconvenience to him.

'*Almost...*' He trials off.

"I will think of you every minute, of every day, until my dying breath, my sweet girl." I bring her into my chest and kiss the top of her head. I feel it then, her entire body shaking.

"You must visit your mother as often as you can. I know she will want to hear all about your adventures."

I never thought in my wildest dreams that I would see my baby girl have to lose both of her parents so soon. Especially one after the other.

Looking toward my brother-in-law, I know we have our differences, but I am hoping in this moment we can put that aside.

"Will you take care of my baby girl?" I ask him.

"You don't need to ask, brother." He places his hands on his own daughters' shoulders, giving her comfort. I will regret everything they have been through and what they witnessed here today.

"I love you," I whisper into her hair.

"I love you too." Her small arms squeeze me tight.

I step away, and her arms swing to her sides. She doesn't look up at me, but I know tears are coming freely now.

"Be brave, love fiercely, my baby girl. Until we meet again." She looks up at me now, watching me as I walk over to Flyran.

He sinks down to the ground, making it easier for me to mount him.

Once settled of his back, I brace myself. "Ready," I say taking one look at my Delilah and nodding my head.

"I love you." I mouth, and Flyran takes flight.

I never thought I would have to leave the one place I called home.

It wasn't the land, the hut, or Archurilla.

My home was Mary, it was Delilah, and they were my everything, and now flying away from them... I have nothing.

‘*That's not true.*’ Flyrans' thoughts filter through to mine.

"It is." I reply, "Where are we going?"

‘*We are headed to Vardrian... there is someone I want you to meet.*’

THE END!

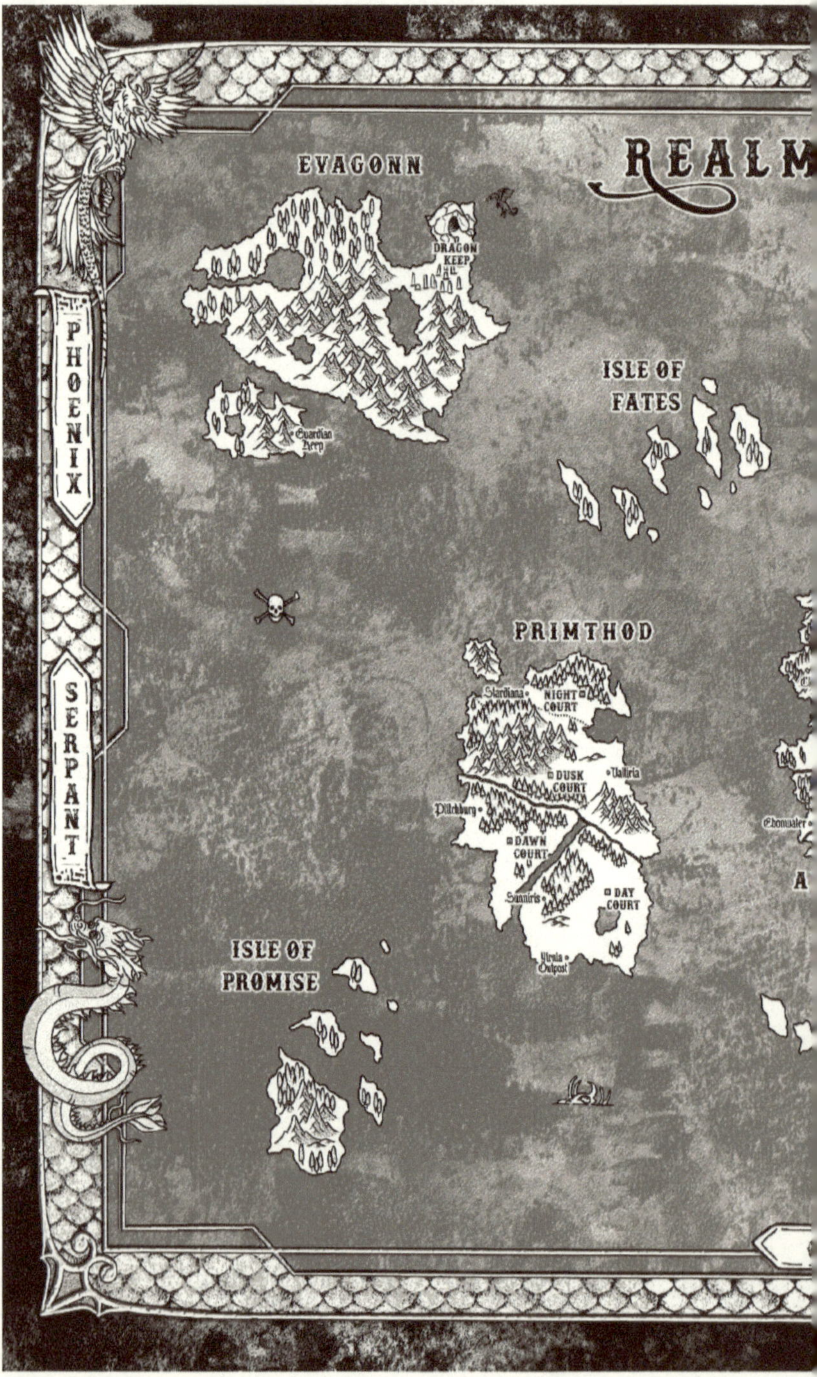

PHOENIX
SERPANT
EVAGONN
REALM
DRAGON KEEP
ISLE OF FATES
Guardian Keep
PRIMTHOD
Stardiana
NIGHT COURT
DUSK COURT
Valliria
Dilchburg
Ebonwater
A
DAWN COURT
Sanniris
DAY COURT
Ytrnia Outpost
ISLE OF PROMISE

AMAROK
IXIAM
WALDARIE
ISLE OF MYXIE
YARDI PRISON
Bloomsburg
Hescadia
SPRING COURT
SUMMER COURT
Oranhvale
LOGOXDIN
AUTUMN COURT
WINTER COURT
Blizville
VARDIRIAN
EDOX
OUROBOROS
N
W
E
S

Acknowledgments

If you've made it this far, thank you.

Thank you for taking the time out of your busy lives to read this book and that I can share my amazing world with you all.

I'm so grateful to still be continuing on with this series.

Fantasy isn't easy to write, I take my hat off to those who write it for a living.

I'm still enjoying writing this world, and the tie-in worlds to come but shh....

Tom, EJ and Harry thank you for allowing me the time to write, to enjoy my characters and their world.

Tom, thanks for letting me rant on about the connections that I had to make, for the characters to make sense and the endless plot holes I created and needed to fix.

EJ, for being my little best friend. Mummy loves you.

Harry for being my cutie little guy. Mummy loves you.

I love you all so fiercely.

Mum and Emma, thank you for your endless support in my passion to create stories.

Beta Babes, Michelle, Anastasia, & Phylicia. Thank you for being there when I needed you!

My street team, I wouldn't be anywhere I am right now

if it weren't for you sharing, commenting and liking my content! I appreciate you.

Monica, thank you for bringing my creatures to life!

Tash, my amazing cover designer. This cover has blown me away, yet again.

My amazing editor Anna, thank you for putting up with me and being my PA for the last few months. I don't think I could have finished this book without you.

To the readers, thank you for still believing in me and taking the chance on this story.

About the Author

Hi!

I am Chloe but my pen name is Chloe O'Connor.

I have loved books since I was little. My journey started with reading the fairy tales we grew up with, to the worlds of fantasy as we got older.

Now, I have dived into creating my own worlds with characters you love, love to hate, and villains we secretly crave.

From dragons to Fae wielding the elements mixed with a little spice, you can't really go wrong!

If you like suspense, historical, murder mystery, contemporary, or psychological thriller, then check out my other pen name ... C. Renee

Please stay in touch at: LINKTREE

This is where you'll be able to find my other titles from both Chloe O'Connor & my other pen name C. Renee.